A Knight T

GO AHEAD, SECRET SEVEN
GOOD WORK, SECRET SEVEN

The Secret Seven are Peter, Janet, Pam,
Colin, George, Jack, Barbara and of
course Scamper, the dog.

This book contains their fifth and sixth
thrilling adventures.

Join the Secret Seven . . .

ENID BLYTON

GO AHEAD, SECRET SEVEN

Illustrated by Derek Lucas

KNIGHT BOOKS
Hodder and Stoughton

*This Secret Seven Two-in-One Special
Edition was first published by Knight Books 1988*

Copyright © Darrell Waters Ltd
Illustrations copyright 1969 Hodder &
Stoughton Ltd.

First published in a single volume 1953
First Knight Books single volume edition 1969

*The characters and situations in this
book are entirely imaginary and bear
no relation to any real person
or actual happening.*

British Library C.I.P.

Blyton, Enid
  Go ahead, Secret Seven ; Good work,
Secret Seven. —— (Secret Seven
bumper double).
  I. Title   II. Lucas, Derek, *1920*–
III. Blyton, Enid. Go ahead, Secret
Seven   IV. Blyton, Enid. Good
Work Secret Seven   V. Series
823'.912 [J]   PZ7

ISBN 0 340 42598 9

Printed and bound in Great Britain
for Hodder and Stoughton
Paperbacks, a division of Hodder and
Stoughton Ltd., Mill Road,
Dunton Green, Sevenoaks, Kent
TN13 2YA.
(Editorial Office: 47 Bedford Square,
London WC1B 3DP) by
Cox & Wyman Ltd., Reading

GO AHEAD,
SECRET SEVEN

CONTENTS

One
Susie is most annoying

PETER was going home from school one afternoon, swinging his satchel, when someone came running behind him and bumped into him.

He dropped his bag and almost fell over. He looked round crossly, expecting it to be George or Colin. But it wasn't. It was Susie with her cheeky face, standing by the kerb grinning at him.

'Sorry!' she said. 'You were in my way. How's the Secret Seven Society going?'

'You just look where you're going, Susie,' said Peter, picking up his bag. 'As for the Secret Seven, it's no business of *yours*. You're always trying to interfere!'

'Jack says there haven't been any Secret Seven meetings for ages,' said Susie, walking beside Peter, much to his annoyance. Susie was the most aggravating girl he knew.

Jack was Susie's brother, and a member of the Secret Seven. Peter was quite sure he hadn't said anything about the meetings. But Susie was right. They hadn't had any meetings for a long time. The Easter term had been rather exciting so far, and Peter hadn't thought a great deal about his secret society.

'Well, we're having a Secret Seven meeting jolly soon,' he said to Susie, making up his mind very suddenly that they would. 'But you're not coming! And if you try any silly snooping, you'll be sorry. You don't belong to our society, and you never will.'

'I know your last password,' said Susie, skipping over the cracks in the paving-stones. 'Aha!'

'You don't,' said Peter, racking his brains to remember what it was. Goodness – it wouldn't do for *him* to forget it!

'I do. It's Jack Sprat!' said Susie, and Peter scowled at her. She was right. Jack Sprat was the last password they had chosen – a secret password – and here was Susie shouting it out in the road. She saw his angry face and laughed.

'I'm right, aren't I? Yours is a silly society. I know your password, and so do all the girls in my class. I told them. So the next time you have a meeting we'll all be along, shout out the password, and you'll have to let us in.'

'Who told you the password?' demanded Peter. 'I know Jack wouldn't.'

'Oh no. Jack's a most annoying brother. He never tells me anything,' said Susie. 'But when I went to borrow a hanky from his drawer, I found a piece of paper there, hidden under the pile of hankies. And on it was scribbled: "Remember the password – Jack Sprat".'

'You're always snooping about, Susie!' said Peter, angrily. 'I never knew such a girl. Why can't you leave us alone, and not keep trying to find out our passwords and what we're doing?'

'Well, why don't you let me belong?' demanded Susie. 'You let Janet belong, and Pam and Barbara.'

'Don't be silly. It's the Secret *Seven*. We can't have

any more members, or we'd be eight,' said Peter. 'Anyway, we don't want you, Susie.'

'You're mean,' said Susie. 'Well, I'll tell Jack you're having another meeting soon. When shall I say it is?'

'Don't you go telling Jack anything!' said Peter, really exasperated with this annoying sister of Jack's. '*I* send out notices of meetings, not you. And you needn't bother to remember the password. I shall choose another one immediately, and let the members know.'

'Oh, well, Jack is sure to write it down to remember it again,' said Susie, skipping off. 'And I shall be sure to find it. Goodbye, and give my love to Jack Sprat.'

Peter glared at Susie's back. What an awful girl! He was glad that his own sister, Janet, wasn't like Susie. He walked home with a solemn face.

Certainly a meeting must be called soon. There hadn't been one for ages. It would never do to let the Secret Seven come to an end just because there weren't any meetings, or anything special happening.

But you can't solve mysteries and things unless there are some to solve, thought Peter. We'll have to think up something else to do, till one comes along. Sometimes it seems as if nothing happens for ages and ages. I'll have to change the password, too. Fancy Jack being such an ass as to write down the password in case he forgot it. He might have known that Susie would find it.

He went home, thinking hard. Janet, his sister, was already there, and Scamper, the golden spaniel, came rushing out to greet him, barking with joy.

'Hallo, Scamper! Been a good dog today?' said Peter, fondling the long, silky ears. 'Eaten all your dinner? Been sniffing for rabbits? Barked at the dustman? You have? Ah, you're a *very* good dog, then!'

'Woof!' said Scamper, and raced round the room like a mad dog.

Janet laughed. 'He knew you were coming long before you came in at the door,' she said. 'He sat with his head on one side, listening for about three minutes before you came in. He must have known when you turned the corner up the lane.'

'Janet,' said Peter, putting down his satchel of books. 'We've got to call a Secret Seven meeting as soon as possible.'

'Oh, good! But why? Has anything happened?' said

Janet, thrilled. She was disappointed when Peter shook his head.

'No – except that I met that awful sister of Jack's – Susie. And she's found out the password, and she was jeering at us because we haven't had a meeting for ages. So we simply must have one, and we must choose a new password, too! Get out your notepaper, and we'll arrange a meeting as soon as ever we can.'

Two
Secret Seven meeting

THE Secret Seven meeting was called for the very next day, immediately after school. Peter's mother was told, and she suggested that all the members should come to tea first, and have the meeting afterwards.

'I'll wash up every single thing after the meeting,' said Janet. 'Hurrah! Another Secret Seven meeting. How pleased everyone will be!'

The notes were sent out, and the Secret Seven were thrilled. Jack went scrabbling in his drawer to find the bit of paper on which he had written the password. He found it, but he was *most* surprised when he read it. This is what he read:

'Remember the password – Jack Sprat. No, Jack Horner. No, Jack the Giant-Killer. No – it's Jack and Jill!'

Jack stared at the bit of scribbled paper, frowning. Whatever had made him write all that? He must have been mad. And which was the password? He was sure it was Jack Sprat.

He looked closely at the paper. 'Blow Susie! She's written half of it! She's been snooping in my drawer and found the paper, and read the password! Just wait till I see her!'

But fortunately for Susie she was out to tea. Jack

hunted for his badge, and at last found it. He had been afraid that Susie might have discovered that too. Really, she was the most annoying sister in the world!

The tea-party was fixed for half-past four, after school. Janet and Peter had carried everything down, and the shed looked very gay and cosy. They had a small oil stove in one corner for warmth, six candles stuck here and there, and a box for a table. Janet had put a cloth on it.

Two enormous jugs of hot cocoa stood there, with seven mugs round it. Ranged on a shelf behind were seven plates of food.

'Honey sandwiches, sardine sandwiches – and I hope you won't go for those too much, Peter, you're a pig over sardines,' said Janet. 'Buns buttered and jammed, all in halves. New doughnuts. A chocolate cake baked today. A smashing jam-sponge sandwich, already cut into seven by Mummy. Doesn't it look lovely? Oh – and a plate of mixed biscuits.'

'Woof!' said Scamper at once, and his tail thumped hard on the ground.

'*Your* dish of goodies is on the floor, but you're not to begin your tea till we do,' said Janet. Scamper looked at his own plate and sniffed longingly.

He saw two sardine sandwiches, made of the tails and little bones; one bun cut in half, with just a scraping of butter, but no jam, because Scamper liked his without; and a very large dog-biscuit smeared with potted meat. What a tea for a hungry dog!

'Here they come,' said Janet, as they heard footsteps coming down the path to the shed. She peered out of the window. 'It's Pam and Barbara.'

Rap-rap!

'Password!' called out Peter.

'Jack Sprat,' came the answer, and Peter opened the door at once. No sooner was it shut than more footsteps were heard, and another knock.

'Password?'

'Er – I'm most awfully sorry, Peter, but it's such ages since we had a meeting that I've forgotten it,' said a voice, sounding rather upset. Janet glanced at Peter. Was he going to be cross, and perhaps refuse to let in poor Colin?

No. Peter didn't look at all cross. He opened the door, and Colin came in, looking most relieved.

'Hallo!' he said, staring in delight at the tea. 'I'm sorry about the password, but, honestly, it's ages since we used it.'

'It's all right,' said Peter. 'It was my fault for not calling a meeting before. Anyway, that awful sister of Jack's knows it, so we've got to choose a new one.'

'Rap-rap-rap-RAP!'

'Password!' called Peter.

'Jack Sprat!' said two voices, and in came George and Jack, complete with Secret Seven badges. The door shut. The candles gave a wavering light in the rather dark shed, and everything looked cosy, and rather mysterious. Just the kind of thing the Secret Seven liked!

'What's the meeting about?' said Jack, sitting on an upturned flower-pot. 'Anything special?'

'No,' said Peter. 'Nothing's turned up, worse luck – but we can't let our Society fizzle out because we wait and wait for someting to happen. We'll talk about that later. Pour out the cocoa, Janet, and remember that we all like heaps of sugar.'

'Woof! woof!' said Scamper, approvingly, and got a lump of sugar from Janet at once. She poured out the cocoa, and Peter handed round the sandwiches. Soon everyone was tucking in, and Scamper gulped down his sandwiches and his bun in no time, and then settled down happily to crunch his potted-meat biscuit.

In ten minutes' time every plate was empty. Not even a biscuit was left. Jack sat back with a sigh. 'That was a scrumptious tea,' he said. 'Any more cocoa left?'

'Half a mug each,' said Janet. 'Pass yours up.'

'While we're having our last drink, we'll begin the meeting,' said Peter. 'It's not a very *important* meeting, but we've got quite a bit to discuss and to plan. If this Secret Seven hasn't any particular job to work on, it's got to find other things to do. Do you agree, members?'

'We do,' said everyone, pleased.

'Right,' said Peter. 'Well, I'll begin. Stop thumping your tail on the floor, Scamper, and you listen too!'

Three

A new password – and a few ideas

EVERYONE sat quiet. Scamper stopped his tail-thumping and sat still too, his head on one side. He was very, very proud to be at all the meetings, even though he wasn't a proper member.

'First of all,' said Peter, 'we must choose a new password, partly because Susie knows it!'

Jack was startled. How did Peter know that Susie knew it? 'Yes, she does know it,' he said, and fished the piece of paper out of his pocket, on which he had written the old password, and on which Susie had scribbled her nonsense.

'Look there, she found this bit of paper, with our password on it. I wrote it down so that I wouldn't forget it, and I hid it, and she found it and scribbled on it! But how did you *know* she knew it, Peter?'

'She told me,' said Peter. 'She seemed to think our Society was about to come to an end, or something, and she was so annoying that it made me decide to call a meeting at once. Jack, for goodness' sake don't leave our passwords about again!'

'All right. I won't,' said Jack, looking rather red in the face. 'But you don't know what it is to have a sister like Susie. I wouldn't be surprised if she isn't trying to peep in at the window this very minute.'

Everyone at once looked up at the little window, Scamper too. Peter shook his head.

'No, nobody's about. Scamper would bark if he heard the slightest sound. Well, what about a new password? Anyone got a good idea?'

'Snooper!' said Colin, thinking of Susie. 'That would be a good one.'

'Yes, we'd all remember that because of Susie,' said Janet.

'We'll have to remember the password is *Snooper*, not *Susie*,' said Pam, with a giggle. 'I'm sure I shall say "Susie" if anyone asks me the password next week!'

Jack often felt cross with his sister, but he didn't very

much like the idea of the password being chosen because of Susie's snoopy behaviour. After all, she *was* his sister, and although she was very annoying at times, he was fond of her. He shook his head.

'No. I don't want that password, if you don't mind. I've got a better one. One that nobody would ever think of. What about "Beware!"? It sounds sort of *suitable* for us.'

'Yes; it does,' agreed Peter, and the others nodded their heads. They began to say the password to one another, in hollow, mysterious voices, and Scamper looked rather startled.

'Beware!' Janet said to Barbara, solemnly.

'Be-warrrrrrre!' hissed Colin to Jack.

'BEWARE!' said Peter to Scamper, who got up at once and sniffed in every corner of the shed, as if he had to discover what it was that everyone was warning him about. Beware! Well, he would beware all right, but what of?

'Look at Scamper. He's puzzled to bits,' said Pam, with a laugh. 'It's all right, Scamper. It's just our new password. Well, I don't think *any* of us will forget it. It's a very good one. Beware! It makes me feel quite creepy.'

'The next thing to discuss is what the Secret Seven are to do,' said Peter. 'I suppose nobody has heard of anything peculiar or mysterious or extraordinary that we could look into?'

Nobody said a word. They just looked at one another hopefully, and then shook their heads.

'Well, as there's nothing peculiar to make plans about, we'll have to decide something to *do*,' said Peter.

'I mean, it's been such a long time since we held a meeting, and societies just fizzle out if they're not kept going somehow. We must *do* something to keep up our interest or when something *does* come along, we'll miss it.'

'Yes, but what do you mean, *do* something?' asked Colin. 'We can't *make* things happen.'

'No. I know that,' said Peter. 'But we can put in a bit of practice. We can set ourselves one or two things to do.'

'What, for instance?' said George.

'Well, we could practise shadowing people,' said Peter. 'And we might perhaps have a shot at disguising ourselves, just to see if we could get away with it.'

'Disguising ourselves? But how could we?' said Pam. 'We're only children. We can't wear false beards, or ragged clothes, or pretend to walk with limps or anything. We'd be spotted at once.'

'Well, perhaps that's not a frightfully good idea,' admitted Peter. 'We'll leave that for the minute. But we could practise spotting somebody, and then writing down a very clear description of him, so as to get practice at that kind of thing. It's always useful to be able to describe a thief in great detail, for instance.'

'But how do we know who's a thief?' said Jack.

'We don't,' said Peter, beginning to be impatient. 'We just go, say, to the railway station, and sit down on a seat. We watch the people standing there waiting for a train. We pick on somebody, it doesn't matter who. We look at them carefully, and memorize everything about them. Then, when they've gone, we write down what we've remembered. It would be very, very good practice for observing people.'

'It sounds rather dull to me,' said George. 'I'd much sooner do some shadowing or something. Anyway, I'm not much good at describing anything. I'm always bottom in composition at school. I just can't think of a thing to say.'

'All right, you can do the shadowing,' said Peter. 'Perhaps the girls would be better at spotting people and describing them.'

'Woof!' said Scamper, suddenly. 'WOOF!'

'Somebody's about,' said Peter. 'Quick, open the door and let Scamper out. If it's Susie we'll give her the fright of her life!'

Four

What fun to belong to a secret society!

IT wasn't Susie. It was Peter's mother coming to say that it was getting late, and did they know what the time was? She was very surprised to meet Scamper flying out of the door in the greatest excitement, barking for all he was worth. He was quite disappointed that it was only Peter's mother!

'Oh, Mother, it *can't* be half-past six yet,' groaned Peter. 'We haven't nearly finished the meeting. Yes, I know we haven't done our homework, but we haven't much tonight. Can't we have another ten minutes?'

'Yes. Ten minutes, then,' said his mother, and went away. The door was shut again, and the Secret Seven began to talk hurriedly.

'George, you can do a spot of shadowing, and so can Colin,' said Peter. 'You girls can do the observation idea, go to the station or the bus-stop, or anywhere, Jack, you and I will do a bit of spying. We'll find a good spying-place, sit there, and watch what goes on without being seen. It will be good practice for when we *really* have to do it!'

'How do we do the shadowing?' asked George. 'We'd be seen following anybody in broad daylight.'

'Well, do it when it's dark, then,' said Peter. 'But don't go shadowing anyone together, you and Colin, or you'll be spotted at once. That would be silly. Go separately, choose someone you see, and follow them to their home without being seen. If you can do that, you'll be very smart!'

'I'd rather tackle a *real* mystery or problem than mess about practising,' said George, in a grumbling voice.

'I'm the head of this society, and you have to obey orders,' said Peter in rather a haughty voice. 'I've got to keep the Secret Seven going, haven't I? Well, I'm doing my best.'

'Anyway, you never know when we *might* happen on something when we're putting in a bit of practice in these things,' said Jack, cheerfully. 'Things pop up most unexpectedly.'

'We'll practise our observation stunt on Saturday morning,' said Janet. 'I'll go to the railway station. I always like that, it's nice and busy and noisy.'

'I'll go to the bus-stop,' said Pam. 'You come with me, Barbara.'

'Right,' said Peter, pleased. 'Now we've all got secret jobs to do, and they'll keep us going till something turns up. Jack, I'll let you know when I've thought of a good place for us to hide and keep a watch on any goings-on nearby.'

Everyone got up, sorry that the meeting had come to an end. Pam and Barbara offered to help Janet wash up, and all the boys carried in the dirty plates and mugs for the girls.

'Now for homework,' said Peter, with a groan. 'I wish I'd listened better in class this morning. I haven't the faintest idea how to do those sums we've been set.'

Colin, Jack and George said good night, and thanked Peter's mother for the 'smashing' tea. The girls washed up together, chattering at the tops of their voices. They didn't say a word of what had happened at the meeting, of course. Nobody was ever supposed to tell anything that had passed at one of the Secret Seven gatherings.

But all the members thought about it a lot. It was fun to belong to a secret society. It was something you could hug to yourself and think about before you went to sleep at night. Janet looked at her Secret Seven badge that evening when she took it off her dress.

'S.S.,' she said. 'It should really be *five* S's. S.S.S.S.S. For Super, Smashing, Secret, Seven, Society! I must remember to tell Peter that. I'll go to the station on Saturday morning, and watch for someone to describe perfectly. I won't miss a thing, not even the colour of his tie! I'll show the others how good I am at noticing every single thing about somebody I see just for a minute.'

Peter was thinking about what he and Jack could do, too, as he lay in bed that night. A spyhole? Now, where would an *interesting* one be? In the middle of the bush beside the main road? Yes, that would be a good place. They could take note-books and note down the cars that went by. They could put down anything they thought was interesting or suspicious. It would be fun!

Each member was planning carefully what he or she was to do. George was perhaps making the most careful plans of all. He was to go and shadow somebody. Well, he would do it really properly! He would first of all hide somewhere, and watch for somebody to come by. Then he would slip out and follow them, oh, so carefully and quietly! He would put on his rubber shoes.

'And I'll creep behind in the shadows, just like a policeman following a thief or a spy!' he thought. 'I'll be like a shadow myself. Nobody will know I'm there. I'll choose a man with a bag, to make it more real. I'll pretend he's got stolen maps in it, or jewels or something. Gosh, I'm going to enjoy this!'

All the Seven fell asleep at last. What fun it was to belong to a secret society!

Five

A little shadowing

'PETER, when is the next meeting, do you suppose?' asked Janet, on Saturday morning. 'I'm going to the station now, to do my practice for the Secret Seven, you know, watching somebody and describing them, and I'd like to know when I can give my work in to the Society. I'm going to do it jolly well.'

'Well, I'll call the meeting for one evening next week,' said Peter. 'That will be time enough. I'm going off now to find a good spy-hole with Jack. Have I got my note-book and pencil? Yes, I have. Well, good luck at the station, Janet, and don't choose just one person. That would be too easy. Choose three at least.'

'I thought I'd choose somebody we all know, too, if I can,' said Janet. 'Then you'll see if you can recognize them when I read out my notes.'

'Good idea,' said Peter. 'Well, I'm off to call for Jack.'

He set off, and Janet went in the opposite direction, to the station. She passed Barbara and Pam on the way. They were sitting on the bus-stop seat, looking rather giggly, with note-books in their hands.

'Have you begun yet?' asked Janet, in a low voice.

'No. No bus has stopped here yet,' said Pam. 'We're each going to choose one passenger getting out, and wait till the bus has gone off again. Then we're going to put down exactly what we remember about the two passengers.'

Colin and George were not thinking about their Secret Seven jobs just then. Both had decided to do them at night. Shadowing would be so much easier then. They were not going together, of course. Peter had forbidden that.

But when the evening came, only George set out. Colin had sneezed three times, and his mother had heard him. As she knew he caught colds very easily, she wouldn't let him go out after tea!

'But, Mother, I *must*,' said Colin, desperately. 'It's Secret Seven work. I've *got* to do it.'

'Can't it be done another night?' said his mother. 'Surely it isn't absolutely necessary to do it tonight.'

Colin hesitated. 'Well, yes, I suppose it *could* be done another night,' he said truthfully. 'All right, Mother, I won't go tonight. But you *will* let me go another night, won't you?'

So only George went out shadowing that night. He had put on rubber shoes so that he made no sound when walking or running. He had put on a dark overcoat, so that he wouldn't be seen in the shadows. He had even blacked his face. He looked most peculiar!

He stared at himself in the glass and grinned, so that his teeth suddenly showed startlingly white in his black face. 'I'd better slip out of the garden door,' he decided. 'If Mother catches sight of me she'll have a fit! I do look frightful!'

He decided to take a rubber truncheon that he had had for Christmas, to make it seem more real. Now I can really pretend I'm a policeman! he thought, swinging the rubber truncheon from his wrist. It looked exactly like a real one, but was only made of thin brown rubber!

He crept downstairs and out of the garden door. His rubber shoes made no sound. He went down the path to the back gate and came out quietly into the dark street. The street lamps were lighted. He would have to keep out of their radiance.

He went along cautiously, swinging the rubber truncheon. Now then, you thieves! Now then, you spies! Look out, here comes P.C. Rubber-Soles, hard on your trail!

Who was he to shadow? Nobody seemed to come along at all. Wait a minute, was this the bus coming? Yes, it was. Good! It would set some passengers down, and he could trail one of them to his home, wherever it was.

The bus stopped up the street, and George saw some black shadows moving as people stepped down from it. Somebody was walking towards him now, having got off the bus. He would shadow him! George pressed himself back into the hedge, and waited, scarcely daring to breathe.

The man came along. He was a tall, stooping fellow, wearing a bowler hat, and carrying a bag. Good! Suppose there were stolen jewels in that bag! George would trail him right to his home, and he would then know where this supposed robber lived!

It seemed very real somehow, not pretence. The night was dark, the man came along without guessing that a boy was pressing himself into the shadows of a bush, and George suddenly found his heart beginning to thump. The man passed.

Now to follow him without being seen. If he spotted George, then George had failed. But George was certain that he could shadow the man right back to his house without once being seen.

He came out from the bush and began to follow the man, keeping well into the darkness of the trees that lined the road. Down the road to the corner. Round the corner. Be careful now, *creep* round the corner, in case the man knows he is being followed!

George crept round cautiously, his rubber truncheon in his hand, pretending to himself that there might be great danger from a fierce thief!

He heaved a sigh of relief. There was the man, half-way down the road. George trotted on after him. Look behind you, George, as well as in front. Quick, George, look behind you!

Six

A shock for poor George

But George didn't look behind him. He only looked in front, and followed the man steadily. Once, when he stopped to light a cigarette, George darted into a nearby gate, afraid that the man might turn and see him.

He crept out after half a minute, and saw the man walking on again, swinging his bag. After him went George, deciding to get a little nearer, so that he could see exactly where the man lived when he went into his house.

So he crept quite near, feeling very bold and successful. And then suddenly something happened.

George heard sudden footsteps behind him, and then a heavy hand fell on his shoulder and a sharp voice spoke loudly.

'And what do you think *you* are doing, creeping along in the dark after that gentleman in front? What's this you've got on your wrist? A truncheon! Don't tell me you meant to use it, you wicked little scoundrel!'

George was so astounded that he couldn't say a word. He stared up at the man, who dragged him to a nearby lamp-post.

'Is your face blacked, or are you dark-skinned?' said the man.

He was a young fellow, strong and determined-looking, and he gave George a sudden shake.

'Have you lost your tongue?' He dabbed at George's

face, and whistled. 'You've blacked it. What for? Are you one of the wretched little hooligans who think they can hit innocent people, rob them and run away?' demanded the young man, and shook George roughly again.

George found his tongue. 'Let me go!' he said, indignantly. 'Of course I'm not a hooligan! I'm only shadowing somebody for, well, just for practice!'

'I don't believe a word of it,' said the man. 'I've followed you right from the bus, you little wretch! I watched you hiding here and there, creeping round the corners, following that old fellow with the bag. Come along with me. I'll take you to the police-station. You can tell your tale there!'

George was really frightened now. He tried to wriggle away, but the man held him too tightly.

'Please don't take me to the police-station,' begged George. 'My mother would be so upset. Take me home. I'll tell you my name and address, and come with you. You'll see I'm a decent boy, not a hooligan. I wouldn't DREAM of following anyone to rob them.'

'All right. I'll take you to your home,' said the young man, grimly. 'And I'll have a word with your father, young man. What you want is a good hiding!'

And poor George had to trot beside him all the way home, held so tightly by his collar that he could hardly breathe.

He didn't have at all a pleasant time at home. The young man made his harmless adventure seem very, very serious. His mother was shocked. His father was angry.

'Well, I didn't mean any harm,' said poor George,

rather sulky now. 'It was only the orders I had from Peter, who is the head of the Secret Seven, our society. We were just practising several things, in case some mystery or other turned up. That's all. I had to shadow someone, and I did. But there wasn't any *harm* in it!'

'I see,' said his father. 'Well, that's the end of the Secret Society for you, George. If I'm going to have you hauled home by a member of the public, accusing you of following some harmless old fellow, and carrying a truncheon, and with your face blacked, well, all I can say is that that Secret Society is leading you into bad ways.'

'I agree,' said his mother. 'He mustn't belong any more.'

George looked at his parents in the utmost dismay. 'But Dad! Mother! You don't understand. I couldn't *possibly* not belong to the Secret Seven. They wouldn't let me go. I *must* belong!'

'That's enough, George,' said his father, curtly. 'You know I won't be argued with. A little more of this and you'll get a jolly good hiding. Go and wash that black off your face, and tell this Secret Society of yours tomorrow that you no longer belong. Do you hear me?'

'Yes, Dad,' said George, shocked and miserable. He said good night in a low voice, gave the young man a fearful scowl, and went out of the room. He debated whether to slam the door or not, but decided not to. His father did not look kindly on any show of temper.

Poor George! He washed his black face, undressed, and got into bed. What a dreadful thing not to belong to the Secret Seven any more! What would they do without him? They would only be Six. Would they call themselves the Secret Six? That would still be S.S.

Or, dreadful thought, would they get someone else instead of him? George felt as if he really could *not* bear that. He buried his face in his pillow and gritted his teeth. It was too bad! He had only done what Peter had told him, and he had done it jolly well too, and that horrid young man had thought he was up to mischief and had hauled him home.

Tomorrow he must go and tell Peter and Janet. They would have to call a meeting on Monday night and decide what to do without him. He would be there for the last time. He would never, never attend one of those exciting secret meetings after that.

'I shall howl if I go on thinking like this,' said George fiercely, and hit his pillow hard, pretending it was the young man who had caught him. Take that! And that!

He felt better then, but it was a long time before he fell asleep. Poor George!

Seven

George resigns – and a new member is elected

On Monday evening, immediately after school, a meeting of the Secret Seven was called. All the Seven knew why. It was about George.

George had gone to see Peter on Sunday morning, and had told him what had happened. Peter was shocked.

'We must call a meeting as soon as possible,' he said, 'to see what we can do about it. Poor George! This is awful!'

So a very solemn, serious meeting was held down in the little shed that had the S.S. sign on its door. George gave the password in rather a trembling voice as he went in, and wore his badge for the last time.

'Beware!' he said, and at the password the door was opened. Everyone was there, Scamper as well.

'Hallo, George,' said Janet, feeling very miserable to see George's woebegone face. 'Bad luck!'

'I expect Peter's told you what happened,' said George, sitting down on a box. 'It was just, well, what Janet said just now, bad luck!'

George took off his badge and handed it to Peter, who pinned it carefully to his jersey, beside his own badge.

'I now resign from the Secret Seven,' said George, in rather a shaky voice. 'Thank you for letting me belong. I'm very, very sorry to go, but my father says I must.'

'It's horrid of him!' said Pam fiercely, very sorry for George.

But George was not going to have anything said against his father, much as he resented being forced to leave the Secret Seven.

'He's not horrid,' he said, loyally. 'It was that young man's fault. He caused all the trouble, making such a fuss about me. He *knew* I wasn't doing any harm. He's the mean, horrid one, not my father.'

'Who was he? Do you know?' asked Jack.

'No idea,' said George. 'I'd never seen him before. When Dad asked him for his address, he said that he lived at that little hotel called "Starling's". He didn't give his name.'

'I've a good mind to go and find out who he is and tell him what I think of him!' said Jack, scowling.

'Yes. That's a good idea,' said Peter. 'I and Colin and you will all go, Jack. It's the least we can do for old George. We'll tell that young man what we think of him!'

'He'll just haul you home too, and get *you* into trouble!' said George, feeling rather comforted by all the interest on his behalf. 'I must say I couldn't understand why he was so jolly interfering. Even when I told him who I was and where I lived, he was just as mean.'

'Starling's Hotel,' said Peter, and wrote it down firmly in his note-book. 'We'll go and ask for him and tell him he's done a jolly mean thing.'

'I'll come, too,' said Pam, bravely; but Peter said no, the three boys could manage by themselves.

'What are you going to do about the Secret Seven

now?' asked George after a pause. 'I mean, you're only six, now I'm out of it. Will you be the Secret Six?'

'No,' said Peter. 'We began as the Secret Seven, and we'll have to go on as the Secret Seven. You can't suddenly change a society as important as ours.'

'I see,' said George. 'Well, you'll have to get a seventh, then. I shall hate that. Who will you have? Lennie, or Richard?'

'No,' said Peter, firmly, and everyone looked at him to see who was in his mind.

'Hadn't we better all put up somebody's name, and then we'll vote?' asked Colin. 'That's if we've got to have someone else. I shan't much like anyone in George's place.'

'You will ALL like the one that I'm thinking of, I promise you,' said Peter, and his eyes twinkled at them. 'Nobody will say no, I promise you!'

'Who is it?' said poor George, wondering who this wonderful person was that everyone would welcome.

'Yes, who is it?' said Janet, puzzled.

'He's with us tonight,' said Peter. 'But he will only be a temporary member, not a member for good, just a temporary member till we get George back again. Because I'm determined to go and find that young man and make him go and ask George's parents to let him belong to the Secret Seven again. I bet he didn't know how important it is to George to belong.'

'But who's the temporary member?' said George, puzzled. He looked all round. 'There's nobody here but us.'

'It's Scamper!' said Peter, and Scamper leapt up at his name, and wagged his tail vigorously. 'Scamper, will you please be a proper member of the Secret Seven till we get George back?'

'Woof, *woof*, WOOF!' said Scamper, joyously, as if he understood completely. Everyone began to laugh, even George.

'Oh, Peter!' he said, 'Scamper's the only person I don't mind taking my place! He's always *really* belonged to the Secret Seven, hasn't he? Oh, I do hope I come back. Still, I don't feel so bad now that Scamper's the seventh member. I just felt I couldn't bear to know that Lennie or Richard belonged instead of me.'

Everybody felt more cheerful. Scamper ran round and licked all the knees and hands he could see.

'Just as if he's saying "Thank you, thank you for this great honour," ' said Jack. 'Good old Scamper! Peter, pin the badge to his collar. Scamper, please remember the password. Let me say it in your ear. BEWARE!'

The meeting broke up. George said goodbye rather solemnly. Scamper took the members proudly to the gate, and then turned back. Wait till he showed the other dogs his magnificent badge!

Eight
A few reports

ANOTHER Secret Seven meeting was held the next night, to hear the result of the various 'observations' and 'watchings'. All the seven were there, but the seventh this time was Scamper, not George. It seemed queer without him.

It was quite a business-like meeting. Janet spoke first. She took out her note-book and read from it.

'I was at the railway station,' she said, 'and I picked out three people to observe as they passed. They came off the 10.13 train from Pilberry.

'First, an old woman with a round face, a big nose with a wart at one side, and grey curly hair. She wore a green coat with a belt, a hat with lots of red cherries round it and . . .'

'Mrs Lawson!' yelled everyone at once, and Janet looked pleased.

'Yes,' she said. 'Quite right. I chose her just to see if I could describe her well enough for you to recognize. Here's the second person, not very exciting. A young woman in a nurse's uniform, golden hair, doll-like face, small feet and a quick walk.'

'Well, it's quite a good *short* description,' said Peter. 'I feel as if I might know her if I saw her. I think you're good at this, Janet.'

Janet went red with pleasure. She loved Peter to

praise her. 'Here's my last,' she said. 'I chose him because he really was a bit peculiar. Listen.

'A very stoopy man, who walked a bit lame, had an old soft hat pulled well down over his face, a long overcoat with the shoulders very square, small feet for his size, a funny hand . . .'

'What do you mean, a funny hand?' asked Peter.

'Well, I don't quite know what was the matter with it,' said Janet. 'It looked as if two fingers were missing, and it was sort of deformed and crooked. Oh, and he smoked a cigarette in a long holder. That's all.'

'Colour of his hair, his tie or scarf, and how did he walk – quick, slow or medium?' asked Peter.

'His hat was too low, I couldn't see his hair, and he had no tie or scarf,' said Janet. 'And he limped a bit. There! Do you think you would recognize *him* if you saw him?'

'Rather!' said everyone. 'Jolly good, Janet.'

'Now you, Barbara and Pam,' said Peter. But their notes proved to be rather silly.

'They sound as if you'd had one of your stupid giggling fits,' said Peter, reprovingly. 'Don't read any more. They wouldn't be a *bit* of use if we were *really* trying to find out something. Very poor, both of you. Now you, Colin. Did you do any shadowing?'

'No,' said Colin. 'I began a cold on Saturday night, so my mother wouldn't let me. I'm doing it tonight, after this meeting. I'm sorry, but it wasn't my fault.'

'Right,' said Peter. 'Well, that only leaves me and Jack. We found a good spy-hole in a thick clump of leafy twigs springing out round the trunk of a great elm-tree. They hid us beautifully. We sat there, peeping through the leaves, and at first we saw nothing.'

'Not many people walk along that road,' explained Jack. 'It's Fairmile Road, and you know how long it is. Most people take a bus. We didn't see anyone for ages.'

'In fact, we haven't much to report,' said Peter. 'The only possible thing of interest we saw was a car that came by, and stopped just near us.'

'But why was that interesting?' asked Pam.

'Well, it *wasn't* very interesting, actually,' said Peter. 'All that happened was that a man got out with a dog, a magnificent grey poodle, fluffy in patches and bare in patches, you know how poodles look! The dog was terribly frightened, I thought. But you could see it was only car-sick and it soon recovered, and began to sniff round quite naturally.'

'It didn't like going back into the car, though,' said Jack. 'It whined like anything and pulled away from the man as hard as it could. He was pretty rough with it, I thought.'

'I suppose the poor thing knew it would be car-sick again,' said Janet. 'Do you remember our next-door neighbour's dog, Peter? Every time it went out in the car, it cried and cried because it felt so ill.'

'Well your report doesn't seem *very* interesting,' said Barbara, rather glad to repay Peter for his candid remarks about her report and Pam's. 'Did you take the car's number? I bet you didn't.'

'There wasn't much point in taking it,' said Peter. 'But as it happens, we did. Here it is – PSD 188.'

'PSD – pretty sick dog!' said Colin. 'That's easy enough to remember!'

There was a laugh, and then a pause. Peter shut his note-book.

'Well that's all,' he said. 'I don't really feel we've done very much that is useful. Janet's reports are the best. They show how good she would be if she had to describe someone seen for only half a minute. The police are always asking for descriptions of persons seen by the public, and hardly anyone ever seems to be able to remember much about any stranger they saw.'

'But Janet would be able to tell them everything,' said Pam, rather jealously.

'The only big thing that has come out of this practice idea is George having to leave the Secret Seven,' said

Colin, gloomily. 'Well, is it worth while my doing my bit of shadowing tonight, Peter? I mean, we don't seem to have done anything much, and I don't want to get caught like George.'

'George should have looked behind him as well as in front,' said Peter. 'You won't make that mistake. I think you should do your bit, Colin. I've a good mind to make Pam and Barbara do their bits again too!'

But the girls looked so crossly at him that he decided to say no more!

Colin got up. 'Well, I'm going on my job,' he said. 'What are you all going to do?'

'Let's go indoors and play a game,' suggested Janet. 'There are five of us left – sorry, Scamper, six – I forgot you! We've got an hour before it's supper-time. Come along in, Pam, Barbara and Jack.'

So they all five went in, and were soon playing a peaceful game of cards. But it wasn't peaceful for long! Who was that rapping at the window?

Tap-tap-tap! Tap-tap-tap!

'Quick! Open the window. I've something to tell you all!'

Nine
Colin's queer tale

'OPEN the window!' said Janet putting down her cards. 'It's Colin! What's happened?'

Peter opened the window, and Colin climbed in. He was panting. 'Thanks,' he said. 'I didn't like to come to the front door or the back, in case your mother saw me and asked me what was up. So I tapped at the window. I saw you inside, playing cards.'

'What's happened?' said Peter. 'You're dirty, and your hand's bleeding.'

'Oh, that's nothing,' said Colin. 'Listen! You know I left you to go and find somebody to shadow, don't you?'

'Yes,' said everyone.

'Well, I didn't see anyone at first,' said Colin, 'and it began to rain and I was pretty fed up. So I chose to shadow the very first person I saw.'

'Who was that?' said Jack.

'A young man with a dog,' said Colin. 'I thought he must be taking it out for a evening walk. It didn't seem to like the walk very much. It kept whining and pulling away from the man, and I thought it might smell me, following quietly along some way behind, but it didn't seem to. I couldn't see what the dog was like at first, because it's a dark evening and raining. Then, when the man and the dog walked beneath a street lamp, I saw it.'

'What was it?' asked Janet.

'It was a bull-terrier,' said Colin. 'A beauty. A real beauty. My mother's friend breeds them, so I know a good one when I see it. Well, I shadowed the man and the dog, and it was really pretty easy, because the man was so much taken up with the dog, having to drag it along, that he hadn't time to notice I was following him!'

'Go on. What happened to get you so excited?' said Peter, impatiently.

'I'm coming to that,' said Colin. 'I followed them down Hartley Street and across Plain Square, and into a little dark alley that led between some big buildings. I went down the alley cautiously, because I couldn't see my way very well, and daren't put on my torch.'

'Was the man there?' asked Jack.

'Let me tell my story in my own way,' said Colin. 'I'm just coming to the queer part. I went right down the alley, and just as I was nearly at the end, I heard the man coming back. I knew it was him because he has the same kind of quick dry cough my Grandpa has, and he was coughing as he came.'

'What did you do?' said Janet, as he stopped for breath.

'I squashed myself into a doorway,' said Colin, 'and the man walked right by without seeing me. But he hadn't got the dog with him. So I wondered where he had put it, and why he had gone down there and come straight back again. So I went to the end of the alley myself and switched on my torch.'

'And was the dog there?' asked Pam.

'No,' said Colin. 'The alley led into a little yard, surrounded entirely by high walls. It was a messy place, full of rubbish. I flashed my torch all round, expecting to see the dog somewhere, tied up, perhaps, or even in a kennel, but there wasn't a sign of it!'

'Where was it, then?' asked Janet, after a pause.

'That's what I don't know,' said Colin. 'I looked absolutely everywhere for that dog. I listened for him, I called softly, but no, not a growl, not a whine, not a movement. And when I tell you that there was no way out of that yard except by that narrow alley, you'll guess how puzzled I was. I mean, a dog can't just *disappear* can it?'

'Woof!' said Scamper, exactly as if he was saying 'No!'

45

'I hunted all over that horrible yard,' said Colin. 'That's why I'm so dirty. And I cut my hand on some wire. But I tell you, there was no sign of that lovely bull-terrier, and no door or gate or anything for him to get out of. Then where was he? What had that man done with him, and why? It just beats me. I simply *had* to come back and tell you.'

'There's something funny about this,' said Peter. 'I vote we go to that yard tomorrow and explore it. If there is some hiding-place there for a dog, we'll find it!'

'What a pity George isn't in this too,' said Janet. 'Peter, do go to that hotel and tell that young man he's got to go and tell George's parents they're to let him join the Secret Seven again. He'll be so upset when he knows we may be mixed up in something queer again and he won't be there to share in it.'

'All right, we'll go tomorrow after school,' said Peter. 'And then we'll go and explore that yard!'

'Yes, dogs don't just disappear,' said Jack. 'I expect there's a kennel there, or something, that you didn't notice in the dark, Colin.'

'Pooh!' said Colin. 'I'll give you ten pence out of my money-box if you find a kennel there. You just see!'

Ten

The young man at Starling's

So, after school the next afternoon, Colin, Jack and Peter set off to go to Starling's Hotel, to see if they could find the young man who had hauled George home the other night and caused him to leave the Secret Seven.

They discussed what to say to him. 'We'll tell him the marvellous things that the Secret Seven have done,' said Peter. 'He'll soon see that a Society that can do the things we've done would only have decent boys and girls as members. I might tell him to go and ask the police about us. They would stick up for us like anything, because we've helped them so much.'

At last they came to Starling's. It was rather a poor little hotel. There was a woman in the hall, and Peter asked her politely if there was a young man staying there. If so, could they please speak to him?'

'What's his name?' asked the woman.

'We don't know,' said Peter.

'Well, what's he like?' said the woman, sounding impatient.

'We, we don't know that either,' said Peter, feeling foolish, and wishing that he had asked George for a description of the man. 'All we know is that he's young.'

'Oh well, I suppose it's Mr Taylor you want,' said the woman, ungraciously. 'He's the only young man staying here. Go into that room and I'll ask him to come and speak to you.'

They went into a tiny room and stood about awkwardly. Soon a young man came in and eyed the three boys curiously. 'What do you want?' he said.

Peter explained. 'It's about George, our friend,' he said. 'The boy you caught the other night. You thought he was up to no good, but actually he was only putting in a bit of shadowing practice. He belonged to our Secret Society, you see, and we do all kinds of things. George's parents have told him he's not to belong, so . . .'

'Well, it's nothing to do with me,' said the young man. 'I can't do anything. He shouldn't play the fool.'

'He wasn't,' said Peter, warming up. 'I tell you, we're a very well-known society here, the police know us well; we've helped them many a time.'

'What rubbish!' said the young man.

'You ring up the Inspector and ask about us, then!' said Jack, indignantly.

The young man seemed rather astonished at this. He stared at Jack as if wondering whether to find out about them from the police or not.

'Well, whether you are friends with the police or not, I'm not having any more to do with your friend George, or whatever his name is,' said the young man. 'So that's that. He's got no right to shadow people, whether in play or not. Now clear out all of you.'

Colin hadn't said a word. He had been eyeing the young man closely, and Peter wondered why. Was he trying to do as the girls had done, and 'observe' someone closely so that he could describe him later?

As they went out, gloomy and resentful, a dog barked somewhere.

Colin turned to the young man. 'Is that your dog barking?' he asked.

'What dog? No! I haven't got a dog. And it wouldn't be any good if I had,' said the young man. 'They're not allowed in this hotel.'

Colin said no more, and the three boys walked out of the little hotel. They said nothing till they were well beyond the gate.

'He's hateful!' burst out Peter. 'Horrible cold eyes and thin mouth! As soon as I saw him I knew he was the kind of fellow that likes to get people into trouble. We once had a horrid master at school who had a mouth just like that!'

'Colin, why didn't you help us?' said Jack, as they walked down the road. 'You never said a word, till you asked about the dog that barked. Did you *have* to be unfriendly like that? You might have backed us up.'

'Wait a minute, I'll soon tell you why,' said Colin, and then the others saw that he was bursting to say something. 'Let's get right out of sight and hearing of Starling's first.'

They walked on a few hundred yards, and then Colin spoke in a low voice.

'That fellow, that young man, *he was the same one I saw last night* with the dog that disappeared!'

Jack and Peter stopped in surprise. 'What! Are you sure? But you asked him if it was his dog that was barking, and he said no he hadn't a dog!' Peter blurted all this out in far too loud a voice. Colin was afraid the passers-by might hear and he nudged Peter's arm.

'Be quiet. This may be important. Don't let's give anything away.'

'It's jolly interesting,' said Peter. 'Let's go to that yard at once and explore. We know the young man is safely at Starling's. He won't disturb us.'

'Come on, then,' said Colin. 'It's just as well the girls aren't with us, or they'd get filthy in that yard. Oh, *blow*! Here's Susie.'

And Susie it was, coming at them like a hurricane, all out of breath. 'Peter! I've heard that George isn't in the Secret Seven any more. Please, PLEASE let me in! Jack, tell Peter to let me be in.'

'Certainly *NOT*,' said all three boys at once. 'We've got a seventh member already, thank you,' said Peter, remembering Scamper thankfully.

'Oh, blow! I did hope I'd be in time,' said Susie, and sailed off at top speed.

'What *cheek*!' said Jack. 'Honestly, she's the limit. Come on, let's go to this yard before Susie thinks of following us. Of all the *cheek*!'

The three boys set off in the direction of the yard that Colin had told them about.

'Hartley Street first,' said Colin, 'then across Plain Square. We come to the poorer parts of the town then.'

It took them a quarter of an hour to get to Plain Square, for Starling's Hotel was away at the other end of the town. They crossed the square, and then Colin looked for the alley-way leading between high buildings.

'There seem to be two or three,' said Peter. 'Which one was it, Colin?'

Colin hesitated. 'It all looks so different in the day-light,' he said. 'I think it's that one. But I'll soon know when we get to the yard. I'll never forget that yard, rubbishy, dirty place it was!'

They chose an alley-way, and went down it. It came out into a small enclosure that had evidently been made into a playground for children. Some little girls were there, riding tricycles and pushing prams. They stared at the three boys.

'Not this one,' said Colin, and they went back down the alley. They chose the next one and went down that. 'I think this is the one,' said Colin. 'Here's the doorway I hid in to let the young man pass!'

They came to the end of the alley and Colin gave an exclamation. 'Yes! This is the yard. I recognize that pile of old boxes, and that broken-down rusty pram. This is where the man took the dog, disposed of it somewhere, and came back without it.'

The boys gazed round. High walls enclosed the little yard. A few dusty windows overlooked it, and Peter suddenly wondered if anyone would open a window and yell to them to clear out.

'Listen,' he said, in a low voice. 'We'd better be look-ing for our ball, or something, in case somebody gets suspicious of us and turns us away before we've dis-covered anything. Anyone got a ball?'

Colin had, a very small ping-pong ball, but it would do! He carefully dropped it in among some rubbish, and then the boys pretended to hunt for it. But really they were hunting for any place where a dog might have been put.

They turned that yard upside down, growing bolder

as nobody disturbed them. It was a very quiet, lonely little yard, completely enclosed, with no outlet but the alley-way, and had obviously been used for a dumping place for old boxes, crates, broken crockery, sacks, sheets of cardboard and other things.

'Everything here but the dog!' said Peter at last. 'I think we've looked into every crate and box, and into every corner where a dog could be, though no dog would keep quiet if it heard us three rummaging about. There *must* be some outlet here beside that alley-way, an outlet big enough for a dog, anyway.'

They had moved every crate and box away from the walls, hoping to find some small door, but apparently the high walls contained no opening of any kind. It was a mystery!

Jack sat down on a big box in the middle of the yard to rest. Colin fell on him in one of his sudden silly fits, and began to wrestle with him, trying to get him off the box. Both boys fell over, and the box turned over too.

'Shut up,' said Peter, crossly, 'That box made quite a crash, turning over like that.'

Colin and Jack got up, brushing the dust off themselves, and grinning. Then Peter gave a cry. He clutched Jack's arm, and pointed down at his feet.'

'Look – see that? What about *that* for pushing a dog through?'

All three were now staring down at Jack's feet. He was standing on an iron lid, a perfectly round one that fitted over what must have been a coal-hole.

'It was under that box, well hidden,' said Peter, excited. 'About the only box we didn't move, I should think. But who would have thought a coal-hole was under it? We didn't really *think* of a coal-hole, anyhow! Get off it, Jack, and let's have a look at it.'

Jack stepped off the round lid, and they all knelt down to look closely at it. 'It's been moved recently,' said Peter. 'It's not as caked with dirt round the edges as it should be. I bet that bull-terrier was shoved through here, Colin; I bet he was!'

'But why push a lovely dog down through a coal-hole?' said Colin, puzzled. 'What an extraordinary thing to do! And it seems queer to me to have a coal-hole in this little yard. No coal-cart can come up that alley-way.'

'But a coal-man with a sack of coal can, stupid!' said Peter. 'Can we get this lid up? I'd like to peep down, and see if there's anything to be seen!'

It was an awkward thing to get up, besides being extremely heavy. Peter got very cross with it. But at last it was lifted, and shoved to one side. Then the boys all bent over eagerly, to look down. Their heads cracked together.

'I get first look,' said Peter, firmly. 'I'm the chief.' So the others let him look first.

He sat back, disappointed. 'Well, it's as dark and black as a, well, as a coal-hole!' he said. 'Can't see a single thing. Anyone got a torch?'

'I've still got mine on me,' said Colin, and got it out of his pocket. They shone it down the dark hole. But even the light of the torch showed them nothing. Certainly there was no sign of a dog! There was no sign of coal or coke either. It looked just a dark, horrible, deep hole.

'Er – anyone like to jump down?' said Peter.

Eleven

The coal-hole

NOBODY wanted to jump down in the least. For one thing, the hole wasn't very big – for another, the dark ground was a long way below – and for a third thing, who knew what might lie in wait for any daring boy dropping down through that hole!

'Well, I must say I think it would be rather silly to get down there, knowing as little as we do about this affair,' said Peter, at last. 'Do you suppose this is where the dog was pushed down, Colin?'

'I don't know,' said Colin, puzzled. 'The dog's not there now, anyway, dead or alive. The hole is empty. I suppose it's really an underground cellar, and may be quite big. Anyway, what's the point of pushing a lovely dog down a coal-hole? It doesn't make sense to me.'

'We'd better put the lid back and go home,' said Peter. 'It's getting dark. I'm not sure I like this nasty, lonely little yard now it's getting towards night-time!'

He took hold of the lid, but Colin stopped him. 'Wait a minute,' he said. 'I've got an idea.'

He put his head right down into the hole. Then he whistled. Colin had a very shrill, piercing whistle that usually went right through people's heads and made them angry. His shrill whistle sounded now, though it could not be very well heard up in the yard, because Colin's head was in the hole. It could be heard down in the cellar, though, for the piercing noise echoed round and round!

'What are you doing that for?' began Peter, angrily, but Jack guessed, and nudged him to be quiet. Colin was now listening, his head still down the hole. He heard something – what was it? Yes, there it came again. Then it stopped.

He took his head out, his eyes shining. 'The dog's down there somewhere all right,' he said. 'It heard my whistle, and I heard it barking, far away, somewhere, goodness knows where.'

'Gosh! Did you really?' said Peter, amazed.

'That was a jolly good idea of yours, Colin. Well, we now know for certain that the dog's down there, so that fellow must have pushed him into the hole. This is a mystery all right.'

'Yes. One that has sprung up all of a sudden, as mysteries usually do,' said Colin. 'What do we do next? We could get down the hole if we brought a rope-ladder, but we'll break our legs if we just try to *drop* down.'

There was a pause. The boys sat back on their bent knees and thought hard.

'The cellar must belong to one of these buildings,' said Jack, at last. 'But which one? It might belong to any of these around us. The coal-hole is exactly in the centre of the yard.'

'I can't see that it matters which one,' said Peter.

'Well, it might,' said Jack. 'We could find out if any firm in these buildings is interested in dogs.'

'Well, I suppose that's an idea,' said Peter, doubtfully. 'Anyway, let's put this lid back now, and place the box over it. We don't want anyone to suspect we've happened on part of their secret.'

They put back the lid as quietly as they could, and dragged the box across it. Now it was as well-hidden as when they had first come into the yard.

'It's almost dark now,' said Peter. 'We'd better get back home. My mother will be wondering where I am – and oh, blow – I've not done my homework yet. It's awfully difficult to swot at French verbs when you're thinking out a mystery all the time.'

'Look!' said Jack, as they turned to leave the yard. 'Look! Only one of these buildings has a lighted window. Do you suppose the coal-cellar belongs to that one? Do you think there's anyone looking after that bull-terrier? He must be scared stiff if he's all by himself.'

The boys stared up at the lighted window.

'It's the building on the left,' said Peter. 'It will be just round the corner of the block. Let's go that way and see what firm uses it. It might be a help, though, of course, the lighted window may have nothing whatever to do with the mystery!'

They left the yard cautiously, went down the dark alley-way, and out into the street. They walked round the block, and came to the building that they thought must have shown the lighted window. Colin switched his torch on to the dirty brass plate in the main doorway.

'Alliance of Callinated Sack Manufacturers!' he read. 'What on earth does that mean? Anyway, by the look of the building, the sack manufacturers must have gone west long ago. What a desolate, dirty place! It hasn't had a touch of paint for years!'

'It may be one of the buildings that the Council plan to pull down,' said Jack. 'I know some of them round about here are being pulled down, they're so old. Come on, let's go.'

'Look!' said Peter suddenly, and pulled the others to one side. 'The door's opening!'

Sure enough it was. The boys stood quietly in the shadows, waiting. Someone came out and shut the door softly. He went down the few steps into the street. He kept close to the wall as he walked along, a tall, stooping fellow.

With one accord the boys followed, their rubber shoes making no sound. They knew that a lamp-post was round the corner. Perhaps they could see this fellow more clearly in the lamp-light. Who was he?

'We'll shadow him!' whispered Peter. 'Come on.'

Twelve

Two interesting encounters

THE man came into the light of the street lamp, but only for a second. Peter tried to take in everything at one glance. He suddenly thought that Janet would have been very, very good at that!

The man went past the lamp, and into the darkness again.

Couldn't see very much, really, thought Peter. He had his hat pulled so well down over his face. He seems to limp a bit. Blow, I'd never recognize him again!

The man got along pretty quickly. He was making for the bus-stop. It was easy for the boys to shadow him, because now other people were walking in the street too.

'He's making for the bus-stop,' said Colin.

'We'll see which bus he catches. Shall we get on it, and look at him more carefully?'

'Yes,' said Peter, forgetting the lateness of the evening, forgetting his homework, in fact forgetting everything except for the excitement of the moment. They were on the track of a new mystery. How could anyone stop in the middle of it and go home!

The man made for the second of the two buses that were standing at the stop.

'It's the bus for Pilberry,' said Peter. 'Come on, we'll get on too.'

The man put out his hand to the bus-rail and swung

himself up. Other people followed. The boys began to get on too, but the conductor put out his arm.

'Sorry,' he said. 'Full up!'

He rang the bell, and the bus rumbled off.

'Blow!' said Peter, disappointed. 'We might have been able to shadow him all the way home.'

'Well, I don't expect he's anything to do with the dog affair, really,' said Colin. 'We might have gone on a real wild-goose chase, and found he was just a harmless old businessman, catching a bus home.'

'Peter! Colin! Did you notice his hand?' said Jack, in a voice suddenly bubbling with excitement. 'When he put it out to take hold of the bus-rail?'

'No. Why?' said both boys at once.

'Well, he had two fingers missing, and the hand was crooked,' said Jack. 'Don't you remember Janet's report, don't you re—?'

'Gosh, yes!' said Peter. 'That man she described getting off the train from Pilberry, at the station on Saturday morning! Hat well pulled down over his eyes, he walked a bit lame, a funny hand . . .'

'And very square shoulders,' said Colin. 'It all fits. He's the same man. But wait a bit, there's nothing extraordinary about us seeing the same man as Janet saw, is there? I mean, it's only just chance, and doesn't *mean* anything.'

'No, you're right. It doesn't really mean anything,' said Jack, his excitement fading. 'It just seemed queer, that's all. Perhaps we're making a mountain out of a mole-hill – he's just an ordinary fellow going home.

They turned to walk across the square again, and

passed the little alley-way that led to the yard. Someone came out of it briskly, and almost bumped into them.

It was too dark to see what the man was like, but he soon passed under a lamp-post, and something swinging from his hand caught Jack's eye.

'Look, a dog-lead,' he said, in a low voice. 'But no dog! It's the same fellow who lives at Starling's Hotel.'

'The one I saw with the dog yesterday!' said Colin, excited. 'What's he doing here again? Has he taken another dog into that yard and pushed it down the coal-hole? Gosh! This is all very peculiar, isn't it? What *is* going on?'

They went on, keeping well behind the young man. He went round a corner, and vanished from sight. The boys went round the corner too, and then got a sudden shock.

The young man came out from a doorway as they passed and caught hold of Colin and Peter by the shoulder. He flashed a torch in their faces.

'Ha – it's you three, is it?' he said. 'Members of the famous Secret Shadowing Gang, or whatever you call yourselves! I *thought* you were following me! Look here, I took that fourth boy, what's his name, George, to his parents, and got him punished for this idiotic following of people at night. And I've a good mind to take you to the police, the three of you, and hand you over for making yourselves a nuisance by doing the same thing!'

'All right,' said Peter, at once. 'Take us to the police. We don't mind. Go on, take us!'

The young man hesitated. He evidently hadn't

thought that Peter would challenge him like that. The boys stood there, scowling. Colin suddenly asked a question.

'Where's your dog?'

'What do you mean? I haven't a dog!' said the young man, angrily. 'You seem to have got dogs on your mind. You asked me that when you came to see me this afternoon.'

'Well, why the dog lead, if you haven't a dog?' said Colin, pointing to it.

'Look here, who do you think you are, asking foolish questions, interfering, following people? And what's all this about dogs? What's on your mind?'

The boys didn't answer that question. 'Are you going to take us to the police or not?' said Jack. 'We're ready, if you are. You can tell them anything you like. But we might tell them a few things too.'

'Pah!' said the young man, looking as if he would like to lash out with the dog-lead at the boys. 'I've had enough of you. Clear off home, and don't let me see you again!'

Off he went with angry steps. 'Well!' said Peter, staring after him. 'He certainly didn't dare to take us to the police – but why? What a very puzzling peculiar young man!'

All these exciting happenings made it necessary to call another Secret Seven meeting as soon as possible. The members simply *must* talk over everything, and try to sort things out. So, before afternoon school on Thursday, Peter called a half-hour meeting.

'What a pity old George is out of it!' said Janet. 'He would so love to hear all that's happening.'

'I don't see why we can't tell him,' said Jack. 'He can't come to the meeting, of course, but I can't for the life of me see why we shouldn't tell him all that happens. After all, it was *his* first shadowing that began all this!'

'Well, he isn't a member,' said Peter, who liked the rules to be kept. 'We ought not to let anyone but the seven members know what we're doing. Otherwise we're not a Secret Society.'

'Woof,' said Scamper, thumping his tail on the floor of the shed. He seemed to think that he had to make some remark about everything, now that he was a proper member.

'Let's put it to the vote,' said Janet. 'I like rules being kept too, but it isn't George's fault he's out of this. I feel as if he really does still belong to us.'

So they put it to the vote, and fortunately everyone was of the same mind. George should certainly be told everything that happened. It would make up to him a little for being out of the Society. Scamper said 'Woof' so loudly when he was asked that everyone took it for 'Yes'. So it was solemnly recorded that the whole of the Secret Seven thought it right and proper to keep George up to date in the doings of the Society.

A very exciting discussion was held. Everyone wanted to talk at once, so Peter became very strict and insisted that only one person should speak at a time.

It was decided that the old man, who came out of the lighted-window building and got on the bus, was the same one that Janet had seen at the station.

'He probably lives at Pilberry,' said Janet. 'I saw him getting off the train from Pilberry, and you saw him getting on the bus for Pilberry. Though I can't see that it's at all important to know where he lives. He may not have anything to do with this affair at all.'

'That's what we said,' said Jack. 'But we feel he *might* have something to do with it, so we'll keep our eyes open for him and his doings. Your description was so jolly good, Janet, that we all recognised him for the man you saw!'

Janet was pleased, Pam and Barbara wished heartily that they had not had giggling fits at the bus-stop, but had noticed people as carefully as Janet had. Well, they would do better the next time!

The coal-hole was well and truly discussed.

'It's pretty certain that for some reason that young man takes dogs there secretly at night, and puts them through the hole,' said Colin. 'Then he leaves them. Do you suppose somebody is down there, waiting to receive them? I mean, somebody *must* look after them, surely?'

'Yes. But WHY are they taken there and hidden?' said Jack. 'That's what *I* want to know. I feel jolly sorry for the dogs. We ought to get the R.S.P.C.A. after them. It's cruel to push dogs through coal-holes and leave them there in the darkness. For all we know they have no food or drink.'

'There wouldn't be any sense in starving them,' said Peter. 'The dogs must be stolen ones. That's quite clear. We've seen one of them. You, Colin, said it was a fine bull-terrier, so it was probably a very valuable dog, and would fetch a good deal of money.'

'Yes, and the one that fellow must have taken last night, when we bumped into him, would have been some other kind of valuable dog, too,' said Jack. 'Gosh! Do you suppose that cellar is full of pure-bred dogs, all stolen? We'll have to do something about this!'

'Poor dogs!' said Pam. 'What happens to them down in the cellar? I do, do hope there's somebody there to see to them.'

There was a silence. Everyone was thinking the same thing. Something had got to be done about those dogs! Somehow that cellar had to be explored!

Colin, Pam and Jack began to talk loudly at the same time, and Peter rapped on the box in front of him.

'Silence! I've said you've got to talk one at a time.

Has anyone any suggestions? Pam, what have you got to say?'

'Well, I've got rather a good idea,' said Pam. 'Can't we look up the Lost and Found advertisements in the newspapers, and see if many dogs are advertised as lost or stolen?'

'Yes. *Very* good idea,' said Peter, and Pam felt pleased. 'We'll do that.'

'And couldn't we go to the police-station and look at the notices outside too?' asked Jack. 'They often have posters giving particulars of lost animals.'

'Excellent,' said Peter. 'Any more ideas? '

'We *must* explore that cellar,' said Colin. 'I did wonder if we should try to get into that building with the lighted window and see if its cellar led to that coal-hole – but we might get into awful trouble if we got in there. Isn't it called "Breaking in" or something?'

'Yes. We can't do that,' said Peter, firmly. 'We can't *possibly* do wrong things in order to put something right. We'll have to explore the coal-hole, but I can't see that it matters doing that. Now, we'd better make plans.'

'Everybody's got to do something!' said Jack. 'Give us our jobs, Peter, and we'll do them. Hurrah – the Secret Seven is going full speed again!'

Thirteen
Jobs for everyone

PETER gave each one of them a job to do. 'Pam and
Barbara, hunt through every paper you can get hold of
and find out if there are many valuable dogs advertised
as lost or stolen,' he said.

'Yes, Peter,' said the two girls.

'And mind you do your job properly this time,' said
Peter, sternly. 'Janet, you can go and look outside the
police-station and see if there are any notices there, and,
as it's fairly near George's house, you can go and tell him
all the latest news. He didn't come to school today, because he has a cough, so he'll be glad to see you.'

'Yes, Peter,' said Janet, pleased.

'And you, Colin, and you, Jack, will come with me
and Scamper to the coal-hole tonight,' said Peter, dropping his voice, and sounding suddenly serious and determined. 'Colin, bring that rope-ladder you've got. It will
be just right for dropping down into the hole, it's not too
long. Bring torches both of you, and wear rubber
shoes.'

'Yes, Peter,' said the boys, looking and feeling very
thrilled indeed. What an adventure!

'Woof-woof-woof,' said Scamper.

'He said "Yes, Peter," too!' said Janet. 'You understand every word we're saying, don't you, Scamper, darling? Peter, can't I come too?'

'Certainly not,' said Peter, sounding very grown-up

all of a sudden. 'This is a man's job, exploring that coal-hole.'

'Today's Thursday,' said Pam. 'Have you forgotten that you three boys are going to Ronnie's party, all of you? You can't do anything much today.'

'Blow! I'd forgotten that!' said Peter. 'We'll have to explore the coal-hole on Friday, then. But you girls can get on with your jobs all right. Now I think that's about all, so we'll go. We'll just be in good time for afternoon school.'

They all went out of the shed, Scamper too, wagging his tail importantly. Pam and Barbara decided to go after school to the public library, where there were many papers they could read for Lost and Found advertisements. So, much to the librarian's astonishment, they seated themselves there, with copies of the daily papers and of the local papers too, around them.

They made some interesting discoveries. 'Look, Pam,' said Barbara, pointing with her finger to two advertisements. ' "Lost or stolen, pedigree greyhound." "Lost or stolen, pure-bred bull-terrier." Why, that might be the very one Colin saw! It gives names and addresses here, both in our county.'

'I've found an interesting advertisement too,' said Pam. 'See – "Lost on Monday, 16th, a beautiful pedigree Saluki. Answers to name of Sally." That's in our county too. It looks as if somebody is at work, stealing pedigree dogs!'

'Here's another,' said Barbara. ' "Believed stolen, pure-bred Alsatian, well-trained, answers to name of Kip." Goodness! Suppose the boys find them all down that coal-hole!'

'What do you suppose the thief does with them?' said Pam.

'Sells them again, of course. They would be worth a lot of money,' said Barbara. 'Or they might claim the reward offered. See, there's a reward of twenty guineas for anyone finding the Alsatian!'

'I wonder how Janet will get on, looking at the police notices!' said Pam. 'Anyway, we've done well this time. Peter can't tick us off again!'

Janet couldn't go to the police-station till the following day. She gobbled down her midday dinner and raced off. She meant to look at the police notices, and then go and see George and tell him all the latest news.

There was only one notice about dogs, and that was to say that dogs found worrying sheep would be shot. Janet hoped with all her heart that Scamper would never do such a silly thing. She didn't think he would, because her father owned a lot of them, and Scamper was used to them. It would be so dreadful if he was shot.

She glanced at the next notice. It described a man that the police wanted to find. Janet read it with interest.

'John Wilfrid Pace, aged 71. Small and bent. Bald, with shaggy eyebrows and beard. Very hoarse voice. Shuffles badly when walking. Scar across the right cheek.'

'I should know *him* all right if I saw him!' said Janet to herself, picturing a bent little man, bald and bearded, scarred on the face. 'Now I really must go and see George, or I'll be late for school.'

George was delighted to see Janet. He was perfectly all right except for a cough, but his mother was not going to let him go back to school until Monday.

'I've come to tell you all the latest news of the Secret Seven,' said Janet. 'Can anyone overhear us? We know you're not a member now, but we all voted that you should know what's going on. And there's plenty to tell you, George. It's all very, very exiting!'

So it was, and Janet told everything very well indeed. When she left George, he felt rather down in the dumps. All this going on and I'm not in it! he thought.

Then an idea came into his head. 'Well – why *shouldn't* I be in it? Why shouldn't I go to that coal-hole, and watch the others going down? They needn't even know I'm there! I can find it all right. Yes, I'll go. Look out, Secret Seven, I'm coming too, though you won't see me! Hurrah!'

Fourteen

Down the coal-hole!

RONNIE's party was a good one, and the three boys and Janet enjoyed themselves thoroughly. They quite forgot the exciting affair they were mixed up in, as they played all kinds of games.

But one game reminded them of the Secret Seven doings! Ronnie's mother suddenly came in with a tray of all kinds of things. 'Now look well, everybody!' she said. 'There are twenty things here. I am going to find out which of you has the best powers of observation! Look well for one minute, and then I shall take the tray away, and you must each write down what you saw on the tray, as many as you can!'

You can guess who won that competition, Janet! She remembered all twenty, and Peter was very proud of her.

'I believe you belong to a secret society, Janet,' said Ronnie's mother, giving her a box of chocolates as prize. 'You must be one of its best members!'

That reminded the three boys of the exciting thing they were to do the next night. Down the coal-hole they would go, and what would they find there?

There was no time for a proper meeting before Friday night, so Janet, Pam and Barbara hurriedly told Peter what they had or had not found out about lost or stolen dogs. Peter was very interested indeed, especially when he heard that most of them were from their own county.

'That rather looks as if the thieves have their quarters in the county too,' he said. 'And if so, it may be down that coal-hole! I'd like to pay back that nasty young man for getting George into trouble. I'm sure he's mixed up in this!'

It was dark about seven o'clock. The three boys and Scamper met at the end of Peter's road, and set off together. Colin had his rope-ladder, and they all had their torches. They felt very excited.

It was a dark night, and a slight drizzle was falling. The boys turned up their coat-collars. They went cautiously, in case that young man should turn up again out of some corner. They didn't like him. In fact each boy was secretly afraid of him. There was something horrid about his cold eyes and thin, cruel mouth that not one of them liked.

They went down Hartley Street and across Plain Square. A bus rumbled by and a few cars.

They came near to the alley-way. 'Do you suppose that fellow's coming with another dog tonight?' whispered Jack. 'We'd better keep a sharp look-out in case he does. It wouldn't do for him to find us getting down the coal-hole!'

'Well, you had better keep watch while we two get down,' said Peter. 'Then as soon as we're down you can make a run for the hole and get down yourself. I only hope that fellow *doesn't* come – we'd be nicely trapped if he did. He's only got to pop on the lid and we're prisoners. We couldn't possibly lift up that heavy lid from inside.'

This was not at all a nice thought. They went along even more cautiously, keeping a look-out for the young man. But there was no one to be seen near the alley-way. The boys went quietly down it and came into the yard. It was pitch-dark there.

They stood and listened for a while, with Scamper silent beside them. If the man was there they might hear a slight movement, or even breathing. But they heard nothing at all. It seemed quite safe to switch on torches and go across to the coal-hole.

Peter flashed his torch round quickly. The yard was deserted, dirty as ever, and very quiet. There was not even the lighted window to see.

They moved the box that hid the coal-hole and heaved off the heavy lid, and then Peter flashed his torch down. Nothing there but blackness and dirt. Colin undid the little rope-ladder he carried and let it drop slowly down into the coal-hole, rung by rung. Scamper watched it going down with much interest.

They peered down. Yes, it reached the bottom nicely. Colin fastened the top end carefully to a nearby stone post.

'Now, Jack, you go to the entrance of the alley and keep guard till we're down,' whispered Peter. 'Come as soon as you hear a low whistle.'

Jack sped off obediently. Colin said he would go down first. So down he climbed, rung by rung, till he came to the bottom. He flashed his torch round. He was in a big coal-cellar. His feet crunched a little as he stepped here and there, and he guessed that there was still coke or coal dust on the floor.

'I'm coming now,' whispered Peter. 'Look out, I'm bringing Scamper too!' Down he came, and soon stood beside Colin. He remembered Jack, and sent a low whistle to tell him he could come.

Soon they heard Jack's feet above, and then he came down too, grinning in delight. They were all very excited. Peter flashed his torch all round.

'Now, there must be a way out of this cellar. Look, is that a door over there?'

'Yes,' said Jack. 'That probably leads into the other cellars or basements. We'd better go cautiously – and listen hard as we go.'

'Nobody saw us go down, that's one good thing!' said Peter, thankfully.

But he was wrong. Somebody did see them go down. It is true that he could hardly make them out in the darkness, but he heard their low voices and knew what was happening! Who was it? George, of course!

George had done what he had made up his mind to do! He had found the yard with the coal-hole, and he was hiding to watch what happened. Somehow or other, Secret Seven member or not, George was going to be in on this!

Fifteen
Underground happenings

THE three boys down in the coal-hole were now carefully opening the door they had seen. Scamper was at Peter's heels, as excited as they were. Peter wished he didn't pant quite so loudly, but Scamper couldn't help that!

The door creaked as it was opened. There was no light beyond. Peter cautiously flashed his torch on and off. A passage lay before him, leading to a few steps. A closed door was at the top of the steps.

The boys went along the passage and up the few steps and then turned the handle of the door. Would it be locked? No, it wasn't. It opened towards them, and Peter peered round the crack. Still there was darkness in front of them. He flashed his torch round.

Now they were in the main cellars that lay under the big building. They stretched here and there, low-roofed, with brick pillars standing up from floor to roof at intervals.

A noise came to Scamper's ears, and he listened, head on one side. Peter saw him listening, and listened too. But he could hear nothing. Scamper's ears were sharper than his.

They moved forward very cautiously, stopping every now and again to listen. It was very weird to be so far under a building, in the pitch darkness and loneliness of these vast cellars. They smelt queer too – musty and old and damp.

They came to another door – a wooden one – and
now Scamper began to get very excited. Peter had
difficulty in preventing him from barking. And then, as
they opened the stout wooden door, they heard what
Scamper heard!

It was the noise of whining dogs! Scamper whined too
when he heard, and wanted to dash through the door.
Then came a barking and a yapping. Then more whining.

'There *are* dogs shut up here,' whispered Peter. 'We
were right. Go carefully now, for goodness' sake.'

They came to a long, narrow cellar, where a faint
light glowed from a glass bulb. On one side was a

wooden bench, on which cages were set. In them were five or six dogs, their eyes gleaming red in the faint light.

Nobody was there with the dogs. They gazed warily and snarled as the three boys came quietly near, but when Scamper gave an excited, friendly whine, they whined too, pawing at their cages in excitement.

'They've got water and food,' whispered Peter. 'I say, look, there's the lovely car-sick poodle, we saw in that car, Jack, do you remember? We saw it when we were doing a bit of practice, hiding by the road in a spy-hole, watching people go by. I'm sure it's the same poodle.'

'Yes. It is,' said Jack. 'Colin, there's a bull-terrier, see?

79

He's the same one you saw with that young man, I suppose?'

Colin nodded. He was very fond of dogs, and he was already making friends with these, allowing them to lick his hand through the wires of the cages.

'There's a greyhound, and a magnificent Alsatian!' said Peter. 'I bet those are the ones the girls read about in the papers as lost or stolen. And here's a Dalmatian – hallo, Spots! You're a beauty, aren't you?'

The dogs were now all very friendly to the boys, partly because they had a dog with them who was friendly too. Peter stood and looked at the dogs, wondering what to do next.

'Should we set them free from their cages, tie them together with rope and see if we can get them out of the coal-hole?' he said.

'Don't be silly!' said Colin. 'They'd never go up the rope-ladder – and I bet they'd begin to fight if we set them free.'

'Listen, somebody's coming!' said Jack, suddenly, and Scamper gave a warning growl. The boys went into the shadows and waited.

They saw an old bent man shuffling along, carrying a lantern. His head shone in the faint radiance of the electric light above, for he was quite bald. He had a small dog with him, a mongrel of some kind, and he talked to it as he came in a curious, hoarse voice like a creaking gate!

'Come on, Tinks. We'll see if all the lords and ladies are all right. They don't think nothing of the likes of you and me, but us don't care, do we?'

The little dog trotted beside him, and they came to the

cages. The old fellow went on talking in his creaking voice, staring at the caged dogs.

'Well, my high-and-mighty ones, my lords and ladies, you're worse off than little Tinks here. You've lost your own masters, but he's got his. You may be worth your weight in gold, for all I know, but you'd give all you've got for a nice long walk, wouldn't you? Well, Tinks goes for two each day. Tell 'em, Tinks, tell 'em.'

But Tinks was not listening. He had smelt strange smells, the smells of the three boys and the golden spaniel, Scamper! In a trice he was over beside them, barking madly.

The old man held up his lantern and peered at them. 'What, more visitors?' he creaked. 'Come to see the lords and ladies, have you? Wait now, you're only lads!'

Peter came out from the shadows with Jack and Colin. He didn't feel at all afraid of this queer old man.

'Where did these dogs come from?' he said. 'Who brought them here? Who do they belong to? What are you doing with them?'

The old man gave him a helpless look.

'Them dogs, why, they comes and they goes,' he said. 'They comes and they goes. They comes in at that hole and—'

But whatever he said next was quite drowned by a sudden yelping and barking by the dogs. They had heard somebody else coming. Who was it this time?

' 'Ere comes the Guvnor,' said the old man, and chuckled drily. 'Now you'll be in trouble. Likely he'll lock you up in them cages!'

Sixteen
Unpleasant surprises

SOMEBODY came up out of the shadows very suddenly and quietly. The boys swung round at his voice.

'And what are *you* doing here?'

It was the tall, stooping man they had seen coming out of the building and getting on the bus! Yes, hat well pulled down, squared shoulders, queer hand! They couldn't see his face even now, under the shade of his black hat.

The boys, taken by surprise, didn't know what to say. The man suddenly opened a nearby cage, and spoke loudly.

'Guard them, Kip.'

The enormous Alsatian leapt out, went to the boys and glared at them, snarling and showing his teeth. Scamper shrank back, afraid. The boys didn't like it at all, either. They didn't dare to move a step.

The man laughed. 'That's right. Keep still. See my hand with two fingers off? Well, that's what an Alsatian did to me when I moved while he was guarding me!'

The boys said nothing. Peter felt wild with himself. They had thought themselves so clever, getting down to explore these cellars and see what they could find, and now here they were, trapped, and guarded by the fiercest Alsatian he had ever seen. He hoped and hoped that Scamper would not do anything silly. Kip would gobble him up in a mouthful!

The man fired questions at them. 'How did you come here? What for? Does anyone know you are here? Do you know the kind of things that happen to boys who poke their noses into things that are no concern of theirs? You don't? Then you soon will!'

He gave a sudden sharp order to the bald old man, who was muttering to himself in his creaking voice. 'Got your keys? Then lock these boys up in the cages. Kip, bring them here.'

Kip rounded up the boys as if they had been sheep, and hustled them in front of the man. Then one by one the Alsatian propelled each of them into a cage, snarling if they resisted. The old bald fellow locked them in, chortling to himself. Colin saw there was a scar across his face as the man looked up at him. There was no doubt about it, he was the old man that Janet had read about in the police notice! But not one of them could tell the police that the fellow was here, because they were all well and truly locked up.

The dogs were roaming about, growling and uneasy. The stooping man had them under control, though, and one sharp word from him was obeyed at once by any dog. He stood in front of the cages mockingly. Scamper was not in a cage, but crouched outside Peter's frightened and puzzled.

'I'm going now,' said the tall man to the little bald fellow. 'I'm taking the dogs in the car. You won't see me again. It's too dangerous here now. You don't need to know anything if anyone comes asking questions. Just play the idiot – that should be easy for you!'

'I'm afeard of the police,' creaked the old man.

'Well, hide away in the cellars,' said the other. 'It's a

83

warren of a place. No one will ever find you. Let these
kids out in twenty-four hours' time. I'll be well away by
then, so it doesn't matter what kind of tale they tell!
They don't know anything, anyway.'

'We do!' said Peter, boldly. 'We know that all these

dogs are stolen. We know that this bald fellow is wanted by the police. We know the young man who brings the dogs here for you! We know you use the building above this cellar for your headquarters. We know—'

The tall man limped over to Peter's cage. For one moment the boy saw his furious, gleaming eyes and was afraid. Scamper thought he was about to harm Peter, and he flew at him and bit him hard on the ankle!

The man gave an exclamation and kicked out at Scamper. He caught him in the mouth, and the dog fled away yelping, and was lost in the shadows.

Then the man was gone, and with him went the dogs, cowed and obedient. He obviously had some extra-ordinary control over them – perhaps he had been a dog-trainer, Peter thought. The old bald fellow laughed hoarsely at the frightened faces of the three boys in the cages, and his little mongrel dog sat down beside him with his mouth open as if he was laughing too.

'Boys! I don't like boys! Nasty tormenting creatures. I always said as they did ought to be shut up in cages!' He gave a creaking laugh. 'And now here you be, locked in my cages, and nobody knows where you are. Shall I tell you something, young sirs? If so be as the police come after me and take me, I'll not tell them about you. I'll say to myself, "What, you'll take poor old John Pace and shut him up? Aha! Then I won't tell you about them boys!"'

He went off into a cackle of laughter, and then set off with his little mongrel at his heels. The boys were silent for a moment and then Peter spoke.

'We're properly caught. Goodness knows how long we'll be in this dark, horrible, smelly place. I wonder where Scamper's gone. He can't get up that rope-ladder by himself, or he'd go home and get help. I hope he's not hurt.'

'Sh! Listen! There's somebody else coming!' said Colin. 'I heard something, I'm sure. Gosh! I hope it's not that horrible young man. It would be just our luck if he came along with another dog for the other fellow!'

There was a pattering noise as well as cautious footsteps. Was it that young man and a dog?' The three boys held their breath as the footsteps came nearer and nearer. Then a torch suddenly flashed out on the cages!

Seventeen

Good old George!

A FAMILIAR voice came to the three boys' ears. 'Peter! Colin! Jack! Whatever are you doing in those cages?'

'Why, it's George! George, is it really you?' cried Peter, joyfully. 'And Scamper! Is Scamper hurt?'

'No. But I say, what's up?' said George, in the greatest amazement, as he gazed at the boys in the cages.

'How did *you* get here?' demanded Jack. 'I was never so surprised in all my life as when I heard your voice.'

'I knew you were coming here tonight, because Janet told me,' explained George. 'And I thought I'd come too, even though I didn't belong to the Secret Seven any more. I thought I'd just watch. I saw you go down, and gosh! I did want to join you. I was hiding in that yard.'

'Well, I never!' said Peter. 'What made you come down into the cellars, then?'

'I waited ages for you to come back, and you didn't,' said George. 'And then I suddenly heard old Scamper whining like anything down in the hole. So I hopped out of my hiding-place and went down the ladder to him. That's all. But WHY are you in those cages? Can't you get out?'

'No,' groaned Peter. 'It's too long a story to tell you, George. You must go and get the police. Wait, though, look round first and see if that old man has hung the cage keys anywhere!'

George flashed his torch here and there, and gave a sudden exclamation.

'Yes, here are some keys, on this nail. I'll try them in the padlocks.'

He tried first one and then another in the padlock on Peter's cage door, and there was a sudden click!

'Oh good!' said Peter, as the lock opened. He pushed open the cage door. Soon the others were out too. They were most relieved.

'Now quick, we'll get the police' said Peter. 'Come on, Scamper, old thing. Fancy you going and whining to George like that! I suppose you knew he was hiding in that yard, though *we* didn't!'

They hurried through the cellars, and came to the coal-hole. Up the rope-ladder they went. They pulled up the ladder and then picked their way through the yard, their hearts beating quickly. Scamper was very pleased with himself indeed. He felt that he had been a first-class member of the Secret Seven!

The four boys and the dog caused quite a sensation at the police-station, arriving dirty and full of excitement. The police sergeant was there. He knew them, and was far more willing to listen to their extraordinary story than the old policemen would have been.

They poured it out, and the sergeant called a most interested policeman to take down notes.

The story went on and on, taken up first by one boy, then another. 'Stolen dogs – the coal-hole – the young man and the dog that vanished – the cellars below – the strange bald caretaker who looked after the dogs – yes, he's the man you've got a notice about outside the police-station. The tall, stooping man – yes, he's got away. He's taken the dogs – in a car, he said.'

'I bet he's taken them in that car we saw the sick poodle in the other day!' said Peter, suddenly 'I bet he has. Wait – I've got the number here. If you could find that car, sir, you'd probably find all the dogs *and* that man too! Gosh! I can't find the bit of paper I wrote down the number on.' He fumbled anxiously in all his pockets but the paper was not there.

'Think of the number. Try hard!' urged the sergeant. 'This is important. If we get that number, we can send out details, and the car will be stopped in a few minutes, no matter where it is. Think.'

'I know the *number*,' groaned Peter. 'It was 188. But what were the letters?'

'I know! Pretty Sick Dog!' cried Jack, suddenly remembering.

The sergeant looked astonished. 'Pretty Sick Dog?' he said. 'I don't follow.'

'PSD,' grinned Jack. 'The dog was sick, so we said the car letters must stand for Pretty Sick Dog – see? That's it – PSD 188.'

'Telephone that number to the patrols cars,' said the sergeant to the policeman. 'Quick now!' We'll get him yet. My word, we've been after these dog-stealers for months. That fellow's a wonder at getting any dog to come to him, then he pops it into his car and away it goes. He hands it to somebody else, who passes it on again—'

'Yes, they go to the young man who lives at Starling's Hotel!' said Peter. 'We know he put a dog down the coal-hole to the old caretaker fellow with the bald head and scar. You could get that young man too, Sergeant. He doesn't know about the happenings tonight! And you can get the caretaker fellow as well. You've only to send men down the coal-hole into the cellar and up into the building above.'

The sergeant stared at Peter in awe. 'I haven't time to

ask you how you know all these remarkable things,' he said. 'Car-numbers – young men at Starling's – stolen dogs and their hiding-place – wanted men – I just haven't time. I can't understand it.'

'Oh, well, we belong to the best Secret Society in the world, you know,' said Peter, unable to help boasting. 'We are always on the look-out for things to happen. Actually, we weren't *really* on the look-out this time. We rather *made* them happen, I think.'

The sergeant laughed. 'Well, make a few more happen. Now you'd better get home. It's late. I'll come and see you tomorrow. So long, and many, many thanks!'

Eighteen

The jig-saw is finished

EIGHT worried and amazed fathers and mothers heard
the strange story of the stolen dogs when the four boys at
last got home, very late, and full of excitement. Janet
heard Peter come in, and flew downstairs from her bed,
anxious to hear everything.

'What! You found the dogs in cages! And oh, how
extraordinary that the man I read about on that police
notice was there! Oh, goodness, were you really locked
up in the dog-cages? And did Scamper, dear, darling,
brave old Scamper, go and fetch George to your rescue?
Scamper, you are one of the very, very best Secret Seven
members!'

'Woof!' said Scamper, proudly, and sat up very straight.

Janet laughed at the Pretty Sick Dog business. So did
everybody. It struck them as very funny. The whole
adventure seemed rather extraordinary now it was over.
It was a curious mystery, a strange little adventure, that
had really grown out of the 'job' and 'practices' that
Peter had set all the members to do.

'In fact, we each had one bit of a jig-saw puzzle, and
when we found they fitted together, we saw what the
picture was!' said Peter. 'We each did our bit, even old
George.'

Next morning there was a Secret Seven meeting, of
course, and will you believe it, George was there too,
beaming all over his face.

'I say, can I come in?' he said, when he arrived, and banged on the door. 'Oh, the password, it's still "Beware," isn't it? It was a jolly good one for this adventure, wasn't it? We all had to "Beware" like anything. I guessed you'd have a Secret Seven meeting this morning, so I've come too. My father says I can be a member again if you'll have me!'

'Oh, George!' cried everyone in delight, and Peter dragged him in at once. 'Did he really? Why? Because we've done such a good job again, and you helped?'

'Yes. You see, the Inspector and the sergeant both came to ask me a few questions, and they told Dad and Mother that all the Secret Seven were quite remarkable people, and Dad never said a word about having had me turned out! And after the policeman had gone, Dad said "All right, George. I give in. You can belong again. You can go and tell the Secret Seven to make you a member again." So here I am.'

'We solemnly make you a member, George,' said Janet in delight. 'Scamper, we told you you were only temporary, didn't we? So you won't mind George taking your place. But you were very, very good as a member, Scamper. Wasn't he, everybody?'

They all agreed heartily, and Scamper looked pleased and surprised to have so many pats and kind words. He gave a little whine as if to say 'Well, what about a biscuit too?'

And Janet, always ready to understand his smallest whine, at once produced a big biscuit from a tin! 'You deserve it,' she said. 'If you hadn't gone to fetch George to the rescue last night, Peter and Colin and Jack would still be locked up in the dog-cages!'

'Gosh! So we would,' said Peter. 'Hallo, who's this coming?'

The big kindly face of the Inspector looked through the little window, with the sergeant alongside.

'We don't know the password,' said the Inspector, sorrowfully. 'Or we'd say it and come in.'

'It's "Beware"!' said Peter, grinning and flung open the door. 'We'll soon have to choose a new one, so it doesn't matter telling you.'

'Have you got any news?' asked Colin eagerly.

'Oh yes, that's why we came to find you,' said the Inspector. 'We thought you ought to know the results of the good work done by the remarkable society you belong to!'

'Oh, good – tell us!' said Janet.

'Well, we got the PSD 188 car,' said the Inspector. 'Got it at Pilberry.'

'Oh yes, why didn't we think of that?' said Peter. 'We *thought* that fellow lived at Pilberry!'

'Bless us all, did you now?' said the Inspector. 'I'm beginning to wonder if there's anything you *don't* know! Well, we got the car, and the dogs. The man has got a shop there, with two or three garages. He'd put the dogs into one of the garages. Goodness knows how many dogs he's stolen and sold. Ah, well, PSD stood for Pretty Sick Driver by the time we'd told him all we knew about him!'

'And we also got the old caretaker fellow,' said the sergeant. 'He's a poor old stick, though, a bit feeble-minded, but clever enough to help a dog-stealer, it seems! We wondered where he had gone to earth, and there he was, in this town, under our very noses!'

'We got the young man too, at Starling's,' said the Inspector. 'He's a bad lot. He and the other man ran this dog-stealing business between them, quite cleverly too. Covered their tracks well all the time, and bamboozled us nicely.'

'But they couldn't bamboozle the Secret Seven, could they!' added the Inspector, getting up. 'Well, we must be off. Thanks, all of you. I wish there were more children like you, you're a grand lot to have in our town!'

The two big policemen went out, and the children shut the door and grinned happily at one another.

'Bamboozle,' said Colin, slowly. 'Bamboozle, that would be a fine word for our next password. What about it? Bamboozle, nobody would ever guess that, so long as Jack doesn't write it down for Susie to see!'

'Don't tease him,' said Janet. 'I do feel so happy, what with George back again, and all! What about a round of ice-creams? I've got my Saturday money today. I'll treat you all. Yes, and you too, Scamper darling! If anyone has earned an ice-cream, *you* have!'

'Woof!' said Scamper, thoroughly agreeing, thumping his tail so hard on the floor that it raised quite a dust. 'Woof!'

So there go the Secret Seven out into the sunshine, Scamper too. I do really think they're a fine Secret Society, don't you? And I can't help wondering whatever they will be up to next!

ENID BLYTON

GOOD WORK,
SECRET SEVEN

Illustrated by Derek Lucas

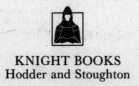

KNIGHT BOOKS
Hodder and Stoughton

Printed and bound in Great Britain
for Hodder and Stoughton
Paperbacks, a division of Hodder and
Stoughton Ltd., Mill Road,
Dunton Green, Sevenoaks, Kent
TN13 2YA.
(Editorial Office: 47 Bedford Square,
London WC1B 3DP) by
Cox & Wyman Ltd., Reading

GOOD WORK,
SECRET SEVEN

Pam

George

Peter

Jack

Scamper

Janet

Barbara

Colin

CONTENTS

One

Secret Seven meeting

'WHEN are the Secret Seven going to have their next meeting?' said Susie to her brother Jack.

'That's nothing to do with *you*!' said Jack. 'You don't belong to it, and what's more, you never will!'

'Good gracious! *I* don't want to belong to it!' said Susie, putting on a very surprised voice. 'If I want to belong to a secret society I can always get one of my own. I did once before, and it was a better one than yours.'

'Don't be silly,' said Jack. 'Our Secret Seven is the best in the world. Why, just think of the things we've done and the adventures we've had! I bet we'll have another one soon.'

'I bet you won't,' said Susie, annoyingly. 'You've been meeting in that shed at the bottom of Peter and Janet's garden for weeks now, and there isn't even the *smell* of a mystery!'

'Well, mysteries don't grow on trees, nor do adventures,' said Jack. 'They just happen all in a minute. Anyway, I'm not going to talk about the Secret Seven any more, and you needn't think you'll get anything out of me, because you won't, Susie. And please go out of my room and let me get on with this book.'

'I know your latest password,' said Susie, half-way through the door.

'You do *not*!' said Jack, quite fiercely. 'I haven't mentioned it, and I haven't even written it down so that I won't forget it. You're a story-teller, Susie.'

'I'm not! I'm just telling you so as to warn you to choose a *new* password!' said Susie, and slid out of the door.

Jack stared after her. What an *annoying* sister she was! *Did* she know the password? No, she *couldn't* know it, possibly!

It was true what Susie had said. The Secret Seven had been meeting for weeks, and absolutely nothing had turned up. Certainly the seven had plenty of fun together, but after having so many exciting adventures it was a bit dull just to go on playing games and talking.

Jack looked in his note-book. When was the next meeting? Tomorrow night, in Peter's shed. Well, that would be quite exciting, because all the members had been told to bring any fireworks they had managed to buy for Bonfire Night. It would be fun looking through them all.

Bonfire Night was next week. Jack got up and rummaged in one of his drawers. Ah, there were his fireworks. And here was his big Humdinger. Jack was sure he was the only Secret Seven member who had got one of those.

'Fizzzzzzzz – WHOOOOOSH – BANG!' he said, and stamped on the floor. 'Fizzzzzzzzzz – WHOO . . .'

'Jack! What in the world are you doing? Are you ill?' called an anxious voice, and his mother's head came round the door.

'No, Mother. I'm all right,' said Jack. 'I was only thinking of this Humdinger and the noise it will make.'

'Humdinger? Whatever's that?' asked his mother. 'Oh, *Jack*! How untidy your bedroom is!'

'I was *just* tidying it, Mother,' said Jack. 'I say, could you let me have some of those chocolate biscuits out of the tin, Mother? We're having a Secret Seven meeting tomorrow night.'

'Very well. Take seven,' said his mother.

'Eight, you mean,' called Jack, as she went out of the room. '*Mother!* Eight, I want. You've forgotten Scamper.'

'Good gracious! Well, if you *must* waste good chocolate biscuits on a dog, take eight,' called his mother.

Good, thought Jack. We've all got to take something nice to eat tomorrow night, for the meeting. Choc biscuits will be fine! Now, what was the password? Guy Fawkes, wasn't it? Or was that last time's? No, that's the one. Guy Fawkes – and a jolly good password, seeing that Bonfire Night is soon coming! Why does Susie say she knows it? She doesn't!

The meeting was for half past five, in Peter's shed, and all the Secret Seven meant to be there. Just before the half-hour five children began to file in at Peter's gate and make their way down the garden to the shed where the meetings were held.

The shed door was shut, but a light shone from inside. On the door were the letters S.S., put there by Peter. It was dark, and one by one torches shone on the door as the members arrived.

Rat-tat!

'Password, please!' That was Peter's voice inside.

'Guy Fawkes!' answered the members one by one.

Pamela was first. Then came Jack, hurrying in case he was late. Then George, carrying a bag of rosy apples as his share of the food. Then Barbara, wondering if the password was Guy Fawkes or Bonfire Night. Oh dear!

Rat-tat! She knocked at the door.

'Password!'

'Er – Bonfire Night,' said Barbara.

The door remained shut, and there was a dead silence inside. Barbara gave a little giggle.

'All right. I know it! Guy Fawkes!'

The door opened and she went in. Everyone was there except Colin.

'He's late,' said Peter. 'Blow him! I say, what a spread we've got tonight!'

The shed was warm and cosy inside. It was lighted by two candles, and there was a small oil-stove at the back. On a table made of a box was spread the food the members had brought.

'Apples. Ginger buns. Doughnuts. Peppermint rock, and what's in this bag? Oh yes, hazel nuts from your garden, Pam. *And* you've remembered to bring nut-crackers too. Good. And I've brought orangeade. Jolly good feast!' said Peter.

'I wish Colin would buck up,' said Janet. 'Oh, here he is!'

There was the sound of running feet and somebody banged at the door. Rat-tat!

'Password!' yelled everyone.

'Guy Fawkes!' answered a voice, and Peter opened the door.

Well, would you believe it! It was *Susie* outside, grinning all over her cheeky face. *Susie!*

Two

That awful Susie!

'Susie!' cried Jack, springing up in a rage. 'How dare you! You – you – you . . .'

He caught hold of his sister and held her tight. She laughed at him.

'It's all right; I just wanted to give your high-and-mighty members a shock. Aha! I know your password, see?'

'How did you know it?' demanded Peter. 'Let her go, Jack. We'll turn her out in a minute. How did you know the password, Susie?'

'I got it from Jack, of course,' said Susie, most surprisingly.

Everyone stared at poor Jack, who went as red as a beetroot. He glared at Susie.

'You're a wicked story-teller! I never told you the password and I didn't even write it down, in case you found it. How *did* you know it? Were you listening in the bushes round the shed? Did you hear us say the password as we came in?'

'No. If I had, Scamper would have barked,' said Susie, which was quite true. 'I tell you, Jack, I heard you say it yourself. You were talking in your sleep last night and you kept yelling out "Guy Fawkes! Let me in! Guy Fawkes, I say!" So I guessed you were trying to get into the meeting in your sleep and were yelling out the password.'

Jack groaned. 'I do talk in my sleep, but who would have thought I'd yell out the password? I'll keep my bedroom door shut in future. I'm sorry, Peter. What are we going to do with Susie? She ought to be punished for bursting in on our secret meeting like this!'

'Well, we've nothing important to discuss, so we'll make Susie sit in that corner over there, and we'll have our feast, and not offer her a single thing,' said Peter, firmly. 'I'm tired of Susie, always trying to upset our Society. Pam and Barbara, sit her down over there.'

Everyone was so very cross with Susie that she began to feel upset. 'It was only a joke,' she said. 'Anyway, your meetings are silly. You go on and on having them and nothing happens at all. Let me go.'

'Well, promise on your honour you'll never try to trick us again or upset our meetings?' said Peter, sternly.

'No. I won't promise,' said Susie. 'And I shan't sit still in this corner, and I shan't keep quiet. You're to let me go.'

'Certainly not,' began Peter. 'You forced yourself in, and you can jolly well stop and see us eating all . . .'

He stopped very suddenly as he heard the sound of panting breath, and running feet coming down the garden path.

'It's Colin!' said Janet.

There was a loud rat-tat at the door, and the pass-word. 'Guy Fawkes! Quick, open the door.'

The door was opened and Colin came in, blinking at the sudden light, after the darkness outside.

'I say, I've had an adventure! It might be some-thing for the Secret Seven. Listen!'

'Wait! Turn Susie out first!' said Peter.

Colin stared in surprise at seeing Susie there. She gave a sudden giggle, and Jack scowled at her.

'What's she doing here, anyway?' asked Colin, most astonished, as he watched Susie being hustled out of the shed.

The door was slammed and locked. Scamper, the golden spaniel who belonged to Peter and Janet, barked loudly. He hadn't at all approved of Susie being in his shed. He knew she wasn't a member!

'Tell you about Susie later,' said Peter. 'Now, Colin, what's all this about? Why are you late, and what's happened? And for goodness' sake, let's all talk quietly, because Susie is sure to be listening at the door!'

'I'll jolly well see that she isn't,' said Jack, getting up, but Peter pulled him back.

'Sit down! Don't you know it's just what Susie would like, to be chased all over the garden in the dark, spoiling our feast and our meeting and every-thing! Let her listen at the door if she wants to. She won't hear a word if we whisper. Be quiet, Scamper! I can't hear myself speak with you barking at the top of your voice. Can't *you* whisper too?'

Scamper couldn't. He stopped barking and lay down with his back to Peter, looking rather hurt. But he soon turned himself round again when Colin began his tale.

'I was coming along to the meeting, shining my torch as I came, and when I got to the corner of Beeches Lane, I heard somebody in the clump of bushes there. You know there's quite a little thicket at that corner. There was a lot of whispering going on, and then suddenly I heard a yell and a groan . . .'

'Gracious!' said Janet, startled.

'And somebody fell heavily. I shone my torch at the bushes, but someone knocked it out of my hand,' went on Colin. 'Then I heard the sound of running feet. I went to pick up my torch, which was still shining brightly on the ground, but by the time I shone it into the bushes again, nobody was there!'

'You were jolly brave to pick it up and look into the bushes,' said Peter. 'What was going on, do you think?'

'I can't imagine, except that there was a quarrel of some sort,' said Colin. 'That isn't all, though. Look what I found in the bushes.'

The Secret Seven were now so excited that they had quite forgotten about whispering. They had raised their voices, and not one of them remembered that Susie might be outside. Scamper gave a little warning growl, but nobody paid any attention.

Colin was holding out a worn and battered note-book, with an elastic band round it. 'I've had a quick look inside,' he said, 'and it might be important. A lot of it is in code, I can't read it, and there's a lot of nonsense too. At least it sounds like nonsense, but I expect it's part of a code. Look!'

They all looked. Everyone began to feel excited. Peter turned the pages and came to a list written down one page. 'I *say*!' he said. 'Here's a list that might be a record of stolen goods. Listen. . . . Silver candle-sticks, three-branched, cigarette box with initials A.G.B., four silver cups, engraved . . .'

Jack sprang up 'I know what all that is! My father read the list out at breakfast this morning. It was in the paper. It's a list of the things stolen from the famous cricketer, Bedwall, last night. Whew! Do you suppose we're on to something, Peter?'

Three

Exciting plans

THE Secret Seven were so thrilled that their excitement made Scamper begin to bark again. He just couldn't help it when he heard them all talking at once. He waved his plumy tail and pawed at Peter, who took no notice at all.

'It must be a note-book kept by one of the thieves, a list of things he stole!'

'What else does it say? I wish we could understand all this stuff in secret code. Wait, look, here's a note scribbled right across this page! See what it says?'

' "Gang meet in old workmen's shed, back of Lane's garage," ' read Peter. ' "5 p.m. Wednesday." Whew! That's tomorrow. I *say*, we *are* on to something.'

Everyone began to talk excitedly again, and Scamper thought it was a very good time to sample a chocolate biscuit and perhaps a ginger bun. Before he did so he ran to the door and sniffed.

Yes. Susie was outside. Scamper could smell her. He growled a little, but as no one took any notice, and he was afraid to bark again, he went back to the good things on the little box-table.

'What are we going to do about this? Tell the

police?' asked Colin, who felt most important at bringing all this exciting news to the Seven.

'No. I'll tell you what we'll do,' said Peter. 'We'll creep round to that old shed tomorrow night ourselves, and as soon as we see the gang is safely there, one of us can rush round to the police-station, while the rest keep guard on the shed.'

It was decided that that would be a good sensible and exciting thing to do. Pam gave a huge sigh.

'Excitement makes me feel jolly hungry. Can't we start on the buns and things? Oh, Scamper, you've been helping yourself! Thief-dog!'

'Scamper! Have you really been taking things?' said Peter, shocked. 'Go into the corner.'

'He's only taken a choc biscuit and a ginger bun,' said Jack, counting everything quickly. 'There should be eight of each thing, but there are only seven of the biscuits and the buns. So really he's only eaten what we brought for *him*, the eighth person.'

'Well, he shouldn't begin before we do,' said Peter. 'He ought to know his manners. Corner, Scamper!'

Poor Scamper retired to the corner, licking his lips for stray chocolate crumbs. He looked so woe-begone that everyone felt extremely sorry for him.

The fireworks brought by the Seven were quite forgotten. Jack's Humdinger lay on the top of the pile, but not even he remembered it – the evening's happenings were much too exciting even for fireworks to be examined. The Seven made their plans as they ate.

'I say, we forgot all about Susie!' said Peter, suddenly. 'We've been yelling out our plans at the tops of our voices. Blow! Scamper, see if Susie is at the door!'

Scamper obediently ran to the door and sniffed. No, Susie was no longer there. He came back and sat down by Peter, putting his lovely golden head on the boy's knee, hoping for a forgiving pat.

'Oh, so she's not there. You'd have growled if she had been, wouldn't you, Scamper?' said Peter, stroking the dog's silky head and fondling his long ears. 'Well, Susie will be most astonished to hear about our adventure when it's over – serve her right for laughing at us and trying to spoil our meeting!'

It was arranged that all the Seven should go quietly to Lane's garage the next night, after tea. Colin knew Larry, a boy who helped at the garage, and it would be quite easy for the Seven to talk to him and admire the cars until it was time to look about for the workmen's shed behind the garage. Then what would happen? A little thrill of excitement ran all the way up Peter's back when he thought of it.

The Secret Seven are on the move again! he thought. What a good thing, after all these dull weeks when nothing happened!

It seemed a long time till the next afternoon. Everyone at the schools the Secret Seven went to was sure that something was up. The Seven wore their badges, and a lot of whispering went on. All the members looked important and serious.

Susie was very annoying. She kept looking at Pam, Janet and Barbara, who were in her class, and giggling. Whenever she passed them she whispered in their ear:

'Guy Fawkes! Guy Fawkes!'

This was very annoying because it was still the password of the Secret Seven! They had completely forgotten to change it the night before, in the excitement of making plans. Now Susie still knew it. They must change it as quickly as they could.

At four o'clock all the Secret Seven rushed home early to tea, so that they could be off again immediately to the garage. They were to meet Colin there at a quarter to five.

All their mothers were astonished to see how quickly the children gobbled their teas that afternoon, but luckily nobody was made to stop at home afterwards. One by one they made their way to the garage. Scamper was left behind, in case he barked at an awkward moment.

Everyone was at the garage at a quarter to five. Only fifteen minutes more! Now, where was Larry? They must talk to him for a little while, and then creep round to the shed at the back. How exciting!

Four

A dreadful shock

COLIN was already looking for Larry, the boy he knew who helped at the garage. Ah, there he was, washing a car over in the corner. Colin went over to him, and the other six followed.

'Good evening,' said Larry, grinning at the Seven. He had a shock of fair hair and a very dirty face and twinkling eyes. 'Come to help me?'

'I wish we were allowed to,' said Colin. 'I'd love to mess about with cars. Larry, can we have a look at the ones you've got in the garage now?'

'Yes, so long as you don't open the doors,' said the lad, splashing the water very near Colin's feet.

The Seven divided up and went to look at the cars near the doorway and wide windows, so that they could keep an eye on anyone passing. They might see the 'gang', whoever they were.

'Look! Doesn't *he* look as if he might be one of the gang?' whispered Barbara, nudging Jack as a man went by.

Jack glanced at him.

'Ass!' he said. 'That's my headmaster. Good thing he didn't hear you! Still, he does look a bit grim!'

'It's five to five,' said George in a low voice. 'I think we'd better go round to the shed soon, Peter.'

'Not yet,' said Peter. 'We don't want to be there when the men arrive. Seen anyone likely to belong to the gang?'

'Not really,' said George. 'Everybody looks rather *ordinary*. But then, the gang might look ordinary too! Gosh, I *am* beginning to feel excited!'

A little later, when the garage clock said a minute past five, Peter gave the signal to move. They all said goodnight to Larry, who playfully splashed hose-water round their ankles as they ran out.

'Blow him, my socks are soaked,' said Jack. 'Do we go down this alley-way, Peter?'

'Yes. I'll go first, and if all's clear I'll give a low whistle,' said Peter.

He went down the alley in the darkness, holding his torch, but not putting it on. He came to the yard behind the garage, where the workmen's shed was.

He stopped in delight. There was a light in it! The gang *were* in there, then! My word, if only they could catch the whole lot at once.

Peter gave a low whistle, and the others trooped down the alley to him. They all wore rubber-soled shoes, and made no noise at all. Their hearts beat fast, and Barbara felt out of breath, hers thumped so hard. They all stared at the little shed, with the dim light shining from its one small window.

'They must be there,' whispered Jack. 'Let's creep up and see if we can peep in at the window.'

They crept noiselessly up to the shed. The window was high up and Peter had to put a few bricks on top

of one another to stand on, so that he could reach the window.

He stepped down and whispered to the others: 'They're there. I can't see them, but I can hear them. Shall we get the police straight away, do you think?'

'Well, I'd like to be sure it isn't just *workmen* inside,' said Jack. 'They might be having their tea there or something, you know. Workmen do have a lot of meals, and that shed's pretty cosy, I should think.'

'What are we to do, then? We can't knock on the door and say, "Are you workmen or do you belong to the gang?" ' said Peter.

A loud bang came suddenly from the shed and made everyone jump. Barbara clutched at George and made him jump again.

'Was that a gun?' she said. 'They're not shooting, are they?'

'*Don't* grab me like that!' said George, in a fierce whisper. 'You nearly made me yell out. How do I know if it's shooting?'

Another loud bang came, and the Seven once more jumped violently, Peter was puzzled. What was happening in that shed? He suddenly saw that there was a keyhole. Perhaps if he bent down and looked through that he would be able to see what was happening inside.

So he bent down and squinted through the keyhole, and sure enough, he got quite a view, though a narrow one, of the inside of the candle-lit shed.

What he saw filled him with such astonishment that he let out a loud exclamation. He couldn't believe his eyes. He simply couldn't!

'What is it, what is it?' cried Pam, quite forgetting to speak in a whisper. 'Are they shooting? Let *me* look!'

She dragged Peter away and put her eye to the keyhole, and she, too, gave a squeal. Then, to the amazement of all the others but Peter, she began to kick and bang at the locked door! She shouted loudly:

'It's *Susie* in there, Susie and some others! I can see her grinning like anything, and they've got big paper bags to pop. That's what made the bangs. It's Susie; it's all a trick; it's SUSIE!'

So it was. Susie, with Jim and Doris and Ronnie, and now they were rolling over the floor, squealing with laughter. Oh, what a *wonderful* trick they had played on the Secret Seven!

Five

A victory for Susie

THE Secret Seven were so angry that they hardly knew what to do. So it was Susie and her friends who had planned all this! While Susie had been boldly giving the password and forcing her way into their meeting the night before, her friends were pretending to scuffle in the bushes to stop Colin and make him think something really serious was going on!

'They took me in properly,' groaned Colin. 'I really thought it was men scuffling there, and I was so pleased to find that note-book when they had run off! It was too dark to spot that they weren't men, of course.'

'No wonder Susie giggled all the time she was in our shed, and laughed when Colin rushed in to tell us of his adventure!' said Janet. 'Horrid, tiresome girl!'

'She's the worst sister possible,' said Jack, gloomily. 'Fancy putting that list of stolen things in the note-book, of course, *she* had heard my father read them out at breakfast-time too. Blow Susie!'

George kicked at the shed door. From the inside came the sound of shrieks of delighted laughter, and some enormous guffaws from Jim, who, like Doris, was rolling about from side to side, holding his aching sides. Oh, what a joke! Oh, to think they had brought the stuck-up Secret Seven all the way to this shed, just to see *them*!

'You just wait till you unlock the door and come out!' called Jack. 'You just wait! I'll pull your hair till you squeal, Susie. I'm ashamed of you!'

More squeals of laughter, and a loud, 'Ho, ho, ho,' from Jim again. It really was maddening.

'There's seven of us, and only four of you,' cried Colin, warningly. 'And we'll wait here till you come out, see? You hadn't thought of that, had you?'

'Oh yes, we had,' called Susie. 'But you'll let us go free – you see if you don't.'

'We shan't!' said Jack, furiously. 'Unlock the door.'

'Listen, Jack,' said Susie. 'This is going to be a LOVELY tale to tell all the others at school. Won't the Secret Seven be laughed at? Silly old Secret Seven, tricked by a stupid note-book. They think themselves so grand and so clever, but they're sure that four children in a shed are a gang of robbers shooting at one another! And we only had paper bags to pop!'

The four inside popped paper bags again and roared with laughter. The Secret Seven felt gloomier and gloomier.

'You know, Susie will make everyone yell and hoot about this,' said Colin. 'We shan't be able to hold our heads up for ages. Susie's right. We'll have to let them go free, and not set on them when they come out.'

'No!' said Peter and Jack.

'*Yes*,' said Colin. 'We'll *have* to make a bargain with them, and Susie jolly well knows it. We'll have to let them go free in return for their keeping silent about this. It's no good, we've got to. *I* don't want all the silly kids in the first form hooting with laughter and popping paper bags at me whenever I go by. And they will. I know them!'

There was a silence. It dawned on everyone that Colin was right. Susie had got the best of them. They *couldn't* allow anyone to make a laughing-stock of their Secret Seven Society. They were so proud of it; it was the best Secret Society in the world.

Peter sighed. Susie *was* a pest. Somehow they must pay her back for this tiresome, aggravating trick. But for the moment she had won.

He banged on the door, and the squeals and shrieks from inside died down.

'Susie! You win, for the present!' said Peter. 'You can go free, and we won't even pull your hair, if you promise solemnly not to say a single word about this to anyone at school.'

'All right,' called Susie, triumphantly. 'I knew you'd have to make that bargain. What a swizz for you! Silly old Secret Seven! Meeting solemnly week after week with never a thing to do! Well, we're coming out, so mind you keep your word.'

The door was unlocked from inside and the four came out, laughing and grinning. They stalked through the Secret Seven, noses in the air, enjoying their triumph. Jack's fingers itched to grab at Susie's hair, but he kept them in his pockets.

'Goodbye. Thanks for a marvellous show,' said the irritating Susie. 'Let us know when you want another adventure, and we'll provide one for you. See you later, Jack!'

They went off down the alley-way, still laughing. It was a gloomy few minutes for the Seven, as they stood in the dark yard, hearing the footsteps going down the alley.

'We simply MUST find something really exciting

ourselves now, as soon as possible,' said Colin. 'That will stop Susie and the others jeering at us.'

'If only we could!' said Peter. 'But the more you look for an adventure the farther away it seems. Blow Susie! What a horrible evening we've had!'

But it wasn't quite the end of it. A lamp suddenly shone out nearby and a voice said:

'Now then! What are you doing here? Clear off, you kids, or I'll report you to your parents!'

It was the policeman! Well! To think they had been turned off by the police as if *they* were a gang of robbers, and they had had such high hopes of fetching this very policeman to capture a gang in that shed! It was all very, very sad.

In deep silence the Seven left the yard and went gloomily up the alley-way. They could hardly say goodnight to one another. Oh, for a real adventure, one that would make them important again, and fill their days with breathless excitement!

Be patient, Secret Seven. One may be just round the corner. You simply never know!

Six

A sudden adventure

NEXT day Peter and Janet talked and talked about
Susie's clever trick. Why, oh why, had they allowed
themselves to be so easily taken in? Scamper listened
sympathetically to their gloomy voices, and went first
to one, then to the other, wagging his tail.

'He's trying to tell us he's sorry about it!' said
Janet, with a little laugh. 'Oh, Scamper, if only we'd
taken you with us, you'd have known Susie was in
that shed with her silly friends, and somehow you'd
have found a way of telling us.'

Scamper gave a little whine, and then lay on his
back, his legs working hard, as if he were pedalling a
bicycle upside down. He always did this when he
wanted to make the two children laugh.

They laughed now, and patted him. Good old
Scamper!

Their mother popped her head in at the door.
'Don't forget you're to go to tea with old Mrs Penton
this afternoon.'

'My bike's got a puncture, Mummy,' said Janet.
'It's *such* a long way to walk. Need I go?'

'Well, Daddy is going out in the car this afternoon. He can take you there, and fetch you back
afterwards,' said Mummy. 'He'll call for you about

six o'clock, so mind you don't keep him waiting.'

The car was waiting outside Janet's school for her that afternoon, with Daddy at the wheel. They picked Peter up at his school gates, and Daddy drove them to Mrs Penton's. She had been their mother's old nurse, and she was very fond of them.

They forgot all about their annoyance with Susie when they saw the magnificent tea that Mrs Penton had got ready.

'Goodness – cream buns! How delicious!' said Janet. 'And chocolate éclairs. Did Mummy like them when you were her nurse?'

'Oh yes, she ate far too many once, and I was up all night with her,' said Mrs Penton. 'Very naughty she was, that day, just wouldn't do what she was told, and finished up by over-eating. Dear, dear, what a night I had with her!'

It seemed impossible that their mother could ever have been naughty or have eaten too many cream buns and éclairs. Still, it would be a very easy thing to eat at least a dozen of them, Janet thought, looking at the lovely puffy cream oozing out of the big buns, and those éclairs! She felt very kindly towards the little girl who was now grown-up, and her own mother!

They played the big musical box after tea, and looked at Mrs Penton's funny old picture-books. Then the clock suddenly struck six.

'Goodness, Daddy said we were to be ready at six!' said Peter, jumping up. 'Buck up, Janet. Thank you very much, Mrs Penton, for such a smashing tea.'

Hoot – hoo – ! That was Daddy already outside waiting for them. Mrs Penton kissed them both.

'Thank you very, very much,' said Janet. 'I *have* enjoyed myself!'

They ran down the path and climbed into the car at the back. It was quite dark, and Daddy's headlights shed broad beams over the road.

'Good children,' he said. 'I only had to wait half a minute.' He put in the clutch and pressed down the accelerator; the car slid off down the road.

'I've just got to call at the station for some goods,' said Daddy. 'I'll leave the car in the yard with you in it. I shan't be a minute.'

They came to the station, and Daddy backed the car out of the way at one end of the station yard. He jumped out and disappeared into the lighted entrance of the station.

Peter and Janet lay back on the seat, beginning to feel that they *might* have over-eaten! Janet felt sleepy and shut her eyes. Peter began to think about the evening before, and Susie's clever trick.

He suddenly heard hurried footsteps, and thought it must be his father back again. The door was quickly opened and a man got in. Then the opposite door was opened and another man sat down in the seat beside the driver's.

Peter thought his father had brought a friend with him to give him a lift, and he wondered who it was. It was dark in the station yard, and he couldn't see the other man's face at all. Then the headlights went on, and the car moved quickly out of the yard.

Peter got a really terrible shock as soon as the car passed a lamp-post. The man driving the car wasn't his father! It was somebody he didn't know at all, a man with a low-brimmed hat, and rather long hair down to his collar. Peter's father never had long hair. Whoever was this driving the car?

The boy sat quite still. He looked at the other man when they went by a lamp-post again. No, that wasn't his father either! It was a man he had never seen before. His head was bare and the hair was very short, quite different from his companion's.

A little cold feeling crept round Peter's heart. Who were these men? Were they stealing his father's car? What was he to do?

Janet stirred a little. Peter leaned over to her and put his lips right to her ear.

'Janet!' he whispered. 'Are you awake? Listen to me. I think Daddy's car is being stolen by two men, and they don't know we're at the back. Slip quietly down to the floor, so that if they happen to turn round they won't see us. Quick now, for goodness' sake!'

Seven

Something to work on

JANET was awake now, very much awake! She took one scared look at the heads of the two men in front, suddenly outlined by a street lamp, and slid quickly down to the floor. She began to tremble.

Peter slipped down beside her. 'Don't be frightened. I'll look after you. So long as the men don't know we're here, we're all right.'

'But where are they taking us?' whispered Janet, glad that the rattling of the car drowned her voice.

'I've no idea. They've gone down the main street, and now they're in a part of the town I don't know,' whispered Peter. 'Hallo, they're stopping. Keep down, Janet, and don't make a sound!'

The driver stopped the car and peered out of the open window. 'You're all right here,' he said to his companion. 'No one's about. Get in touch with Q8061 at once. Tell him Sid's place, five o'clock any evening. I'll be there.'

'Right,' said the other man and opened his door cautiously. Then he shut it again, and ducked his head down.

'What's up? Someone coming?' said the driver.

'No. I think I've dropped something,' said the other man, in a muffled voice. He appeared to be groping over the floor. 'I'm sure I heard something drop.'

'For goodness' sake! Clear out now while the going's good!' said the driver impatiently. 'The police will be on the look-out for this car in a few minutes. I'm going to Sid's, and I don't know anything at all about you, see? Not a thing!'

The other man muttered something and opened his door again. He slid out into the dark road. The driver got out on his side; both doors were left open, as the men did not want to make the slightest noise that might call attention to them.

Peter sat up cautiously. He could not see or hear anything of the two men. The darkness had swallowed them completely. In this road the lamp-posts were few and far between, and the driver had been careful to stop in the darkest spot he could find. He had switched headlights and sidelights off as soon as he had stopped.

Peter reached over to the front of the car and switched them on. He didn't want anything to run into his father's car and smash it. He wished he could drive, but he couldn't, and anyway, he was much too young to have a licence. What should he do now?

Janet sat up, too, still trembling. 'Where are we?' she said. 'Have those men gone?'

'Yes. It's all right, Janet; I don't think they're coming back,' said Peter. 'My word, I wonder who they were and why they wanted to come here in the car? Talk about an adventure! We were moaning last

night because there wasn't even the smell of one, and
now here's one, right out of the blue!'

'Well, I don't much like an adventure in the dark,'
said Janet. 'What are we going to do?'

'We must get in touch with Daddy,' said Peter. 'He
must still be waiting at the station, unless he's gone
home! But we haven't been more than a few minutes.
I think I'll try to find a telephone box and telephone
the station to see if Daddy is still there.'

'I'm not going to wait in the car by myself,' said

Janet, at once. 'Oh dear, I wish we had Scamper with
us. I should feel much better then.'

'The men wouldn't have taken the car if Scamper
had been with us,' said Peter, getting out. 'He would
have barked, and they would have run off to someone
else's car. Come on, Janet, get out. I'll lock the doors
in case there is anyone else who might take a fancy to
Daddy's car!'

He locked all the doors, Janet holding his torch for
him so that he could see what he was doing. Then
they went down the street to see if they could find a
telephone box anywhere.

They were lucky. One was at the corner of the very road where they were! Peter slipped inside and dialled the railway station.

'Station here,' said a voice at the other end.

'This is Peter, of Old Mill House,' said Peter. 'Is my father at the station still, by any chance?'

'Yes, he is,' said the voice. 'He's just collecting some goods. Do you want to speak to him? Right, I'll ask him to come to the phone.'

Half a minute later Peter heard his father's voice. 'Yes? Who is it? *You*, Peter! But – but aren't you still in the car, in the station yard? Where are you?'

Peter explained everything as clearly as he could, and his father listened to his tale in amazement. 'Well! Two car thieves going off with my car and not guessing you and Janet were in it. Where are you?'

'Janet's just asked somebody,' said Peter. 'We're in Jackson Street, not far from the Broadway. Can you get here, Dad, and fetch the car? We'll wait.'

'Yes. I'll get a taxi here in the yard,' said his father. 'Well, of all the things to happen!'

Janet and Peter went back to the car. Now that they knew their father would be along in a few minutes they no longer felt scared. Instead they began to feel rather pleased and important.

'We'll have to call a Secret Seven meeting about this *at once*,' said Peter. 'The police will be on to it, I expect, and *we'll* work on it too. What will Susie do *now*? Who cares about her silly tricks? Nobody at all!'

Eight

Another meeting

In a short time a taxi drew up beside the car and the children's father jumped out.

'Here we are!' called Janet, as her father paid the taxi-man

He ran over, and got into the driver's seat. 'Well! Little did I think my car had been driven away while I was in the station,' he said. 'Are you sure you're all right?'

'Oh yes,' said Peter. 'We were half asleep at the back; the men didn't even spot us. They got in and drove straight to this place, then got out. They hardly said a word to one another.'

'Oh. Well, I suppose they weren't really car thieves,' said his father. 'Just a couple of young idiots who wanted to drive somewhere instead of walk. I shan't bother to inform the police. We'd never catch the fellows, and it would be waste of everyone's time. I've got the car back; that's all that matters.'

The two children felt a little flat to have their extraordinary adventure disposed of in this way.

'But aren't you *really* going to tell the police?'asked Peter, quite disappointed. 'The men may be real rogues.'

'They probably are. But I'm not going to waste *my*

time on them,' said his father. 'They'll be caught for something sooner or later! It's a good thing you had the sense to keep quiet in the back of the car!'

Their mother was a good deal more interested in the affair than Daddy, yet even she thought it was just a silly prank on the part of two young men. But it was different when Peter telephoned to Jack and told him what happened. Jack was absolutely thrilled.

'Gracious! Really! My word! I wish I'd been with you!' he shouted in excitement, clutching the telephone hard. 'Let's have a meeting about it. Tomorrow afternoon at three o'clock? We've all got a half-holiday tomorrow, haven't we? We'll tell the others at school there's a meeting on. I'll ... Sh. Sh!'

'What are you shushing about?' asked Peter. 'Oh, is that awful Susie about? All right, not a word more. See you tomorrow.'

Next afternoon, at three o'clock, all the Secret Seven were down in the shed, Scamper with them too, running from one to another excitedly. He could feel that something important was on foot!

The oil-stove was already lighted and the shed was nice and warm. Curtains were drawn across the windows in case anyone should peer in. Nobody had had time to bring things to eat, but fortunately George had had a present of a large bag of humbugs from his grandmother. He handed them round.

'I say, how super,' said Jack. 'Your granny does buy such ENORMOUS humbugs. They last for ages.

Now we shall all be comfortable for the rest of the afternoon, with one of these in our cheeks.'

They sat round on boxes or on old rugs, each with their cheeks bulging with a peppermint humbug. Scamper didn't like them, which was lucky. The children made him sit by the door and listen in case anyone came prying, that awful Susie, for instance, or one of her silly friends!

Peter related the whole happening, and everyone listened, thrilled.

'And do you mean to say your father isn't going to

the police?' said Colin. 'Well, that leaves the field free for us. Come along, Secret Seven, here's something right up our street!'

'It's very exciting,' said Pam. 'But what exactly are we going to work on? I mean, what is there to find out? I wouldn't even know where to *begin*!'

'Well, I'll tell you what *I* think,' said Peter, carefully moving his humbug to the other cheek. 'I think those men are up to something. I don't know what, but I think we ought to find out something about them.'

'But how can we?' asked Pam. 'I don't like the sound of them, anyway.'

'Well, if you don't want to be in on this, there's nothing to stop you from walking out,' said Peter, getting cross with Pam. 'The door's over there.'

Pam changed her mind in a hurry. 'Oh no, I *want* to be in on this; of course I do. You tell us what to do, Peter.'

'Well we don't *know* very much,' said Peter. 'Excuse me, all of you, but I'm going to take my humbug out for a minute or two, while I talk. There, that's better. No, Scamper, don't sniff at it; you don't *like* humbugs!'

With his sweet safely on a clean piece of paper beside him, Peter addressed the meeting.

'We haven't really much to go on, as I said,' he began. 'But we have a *few* clues. One is "Sid's Place". We ought to try and find where that is and watch it, to see if either of the men go there. Then we could shadow them. We'd have to watch it at five o'clock each day.'

'Go on,' said George.

'Then there's Q8061,' said Peter. 'That might be a telephone number. We could find out about that.'

'That's silly!' said Pam. 'It doesn't look a bit like a telephone number!'

Peter took no notice of Pam. 'One man had a low-brimmed hat and long hair down to his collar,' he said. 'And I *think* there was something wrong with one hand – it looked as if the tip of the middle finger was missing. I only *just* caught sight of it in the light of a lamp-post, but I'm fairly sure.'

'And the other man had very short hair,' said Janet, suddenly. 'I did notice that. Oh, and Peter, do you remember that he said he thought he'd dropped something? Do you think he had? We never looked to see! He didn't find whatever it was.'

'Gosh, yes, I forgot all about that,' said Peter. 'That's most important. We'll all go and look in the car at once. Bring your torches, please, Secret Seven!'

Nine

The Seven get going

SCAMPER darted out into the garden with the Seven.
Jack looked about to see if Susie or any of her friends
were in hiding, but as Scamper didn't run barking at
any bush, he felt sure that Susie must be somewhere
else!

They all went to the garage. Peter hoped that the
car would be there. It was! The children opened the
doors and looked inside.

'It's no good us looking in the back,' said Peter.
'The men were in front.'

He felt about everywhere, and shone his torch into
every corner of the front of the car. The garage was
rather dark, although it was only half-past three in
the afternoon.

'Nothing!' he said disappointed.

'Let *me* see,' said Janet. 'I once dropped a pencil
and couldn't find it, and it was down between the two
front seats!'

She slid her fingers in between the two seats and felt
about. She gave a cry and pulled something out. It
was a spectacle case. She held it up in triumph.

'Look! That's it. He dropped his spectacle case!'

'But he didn't wear glasses,' said Peter.

'He could have reading glasses, couldn't he?' said
Janet. 'Like Granny?'

She opened the case. It was empty. She gave another little squeal.

'Look, it's got his name inside! What do you think of *that*? And his telephone number! *Now* we're on to something!'

The Secret Seven crossed round to look. Janet pointed to a little label inside. On it neatly written was a name and number. 'Briggs. Renning 2150.'

'Renning – that's not far away!' said Peter. 'We can look up the name in the telephone directory and see his address. I say, what a find!'

Everyone was thrilled. Jack was just about to shut the door of the car when he suddenly remembered that no one had looked *under* the left-hand front seat, where the man who had dropped something had sat. He took a little stock from a bundle of garden bamboos standing in a nearby corner and poked under the seat with it, and out rolled a button!

'Look!' said Jack, holding it up.

Peter gave it a glance.

'Oh that's off my father's macintosh,' he said. 'It must have been there for ages.'

He put it into his pocket, and they all went back to the shed, feeling very excited.

'Well, first we find out Mr Briggs' address. Then we all ride over to see him,' said Peter. 'We'll make him admit he dropped it in the car, and then I'll pounce like anything and say, "And what were you doing in my father's car?" I'm sure the police would be interested if we could actually tell them the name and address of the man who went off in Dad's car like that, and probably they would make him give the name of the other man too!'

This long speech made Peter quite out of breath. The others gazed at him in admiration. It all sounded very bold.

'All right. What about now, this very minute, if we can find his address in Renning?' said Jack. 'Nothing like striking while the iron's hot. We could have tea in that little tea-shop in Renning. They have wonderful macaroons. I ate five last time I was there.'

'Then somebody else must have paid the bill,' said Colin. 'Yes, do let's go now. It *would* be fun, but you can jolly well do the talking, Peter!'

'Have you all got your bikes?' said Peter. 'Good. Let's just go in and take a look at the telephone directory, and get the address. Mr Briggs, we're coming after you!'

The telephone directory was very helpful. Mr H. E. J. Briggs lived at Little Hill, Raynes Road, Renning. Telephone number 2150. Peter copied it down carefully.

Got enough money for tea, everyone?' he asked.

Colin had only a penny or two, so Peter offered to lend him some. Now they were all ready to set off.

Peter told his mother they were going out to tea, and away they went, riding carefully in single line down the main road, as they had been taught to do.

Renning was about three miles away, and it didn't really take them long to get there.

'Shall we have tea first?' asked George, looking longingly at the tea-shop they were passing.

'No. Work first, pleasure afterwards,' said Peter, who was always very strict about things like that. They cycled on to Raynes Road.

It was only a little lane, set with pretty little cottages. Little Hill was at one end, a nice little place with a gay garden.

'Well it doesn't *look* like the home of a rogue,' said Jack. 'But you never know. See, there's someone in the garden, Peter. Come on, do your job. Let's see how you handle things of this sort. Make him admit he dropped that spectacle case in your father's car!'

'Right!' said Peter, and went in boldly at the garden gate. 'Er – good afternoon, sir. Are you Mr Briggs?'

Ten

Peter feels hot all over

As soon as Peter saw the man closely, he knew at once that he wasn't either of the men in the car. For one thing, this man had a big round head, and a face to match, and both the other men had had rather narrow heads, as far as he had been able to see.

The man looked a little surprised. 'No,' he said. 'I'm not Mr Briggs. I'm just a friend staying with him. Do you want him? I'll call him?'

Peter began to feel a little uncomfortable. Somehow this pretty garden and trim little cottage didn't seem the kind of place those men would live in!

'Henry! Henry, there's someone asking for you!' called the man.

Peter saw that the other Secret Seven members were watching eagerly. Would 'Henry' prove to be one of the men they were hunting for?

A man came strolling out, someone with trim, short hair and a narrow head. Yes, he *might* be the man who had sat in the left-hand seat of the car, except that he didn't in the least look as if he could possibly take someone else's car!

Still you never know! thought Peter.

The man looked inquiringly at him. 'What do you want?' he said.

'Er – is your name Mr H. E. J. Briggs, sir?' asked Peter, politely.

'It is,' said the man looking amused. 'Why?'

'Er – well, have you by any chance lost a spectacle case, sir?' asked Peter.

All the rest of the Seven outside the garden held their breath. What would he say?

'Yes. I *have* lost one,' said the man surprised. 'Have you found it? Where was it?'

'It was in the front of a car,' answered Peter, watching him closely.

Now if the man was one of the car-thieves, he would surely look embarrassed, or deny it. He would know that it was the case he had dropped the night before and would be afraid of saying 'Yes, I dropped it there.'

'What an extraordinary thing!' said the man. 'Whose car? You sound rather *mysterious*. Losing a spectacle case is quite an ordinary thing to do, you know!'

'It was dropped in my father's car last night,' said Peter, still watching the man.

'Oh no, it wasn't,' said Mr Briggs at once. 'I've lost this case for about a week. It can't be mine. I wasn't in anyone's car last night.

'It *is* the man we want, I bet it is! said Pam in a low voice to Janet. 'He's telling fibs!'

'The case has your name in it,' said Peter, 'so we know it's yours. And it *was* in my father's car last night.'

'Who *is* your father?' said the man, sounding puzzled. 'I can't quite follow what you're getting at. And where's the case?'

'My father lives at Old Mill House,' began Peter, 'and he's ...'

'Good gracious! He's not Jack, my farmer friend, surely?' said Mr Briggs. 'That explains everything! He very kindly gave me a lift one day last week, and I must have dropped my spectacle case in his car then. I hunted for it everywhere when I got back home. Never thought of the car, of course! Well, well, so you've brought it back?'

'Oh, are you the man my father speaks of as Harry?' said Peter, taken aback. 'Gracious! Well I suppose you *did* drop your case, then, and not last night, as I thought. Here it is, sir. It's got your name and telephone number in it. That's how we knew it was yours.'

He held it out, and the man took it, smiling. 'Thanks,' he said, 'and now perhaps you'll tell me what all the mystery was about, and why you insisted I had dropped it last night, and why you looked at me as if I were somebody Very Suspicious Indeed.'

Peter heard the others giggling, and he went red. He really didn't know *what* to say!

'Well,' he said, 'you see, two men took my father's car last night, and when we looked in it today we found this case, and we thought perhaps it belonged to one of the men.'

Mr Briggs laughed. 'I see, doing a little detective work. Well, it's very disappointing for you, but I don't happen to be a car-thief. Look, here's twenty pence for bringing back my case. Buy some chocolate and share it with those interested friends of yours watching over the hedge.'

'Oh no, thank you, sir,' said Peter, backing away. 'I don't want anything. I'm only too glad to bring your case back. Goodbye, sir!'

He went quickly out of the garden, most relieved to get away from the amused eyes of Mr Briggs. Goodness, what a mistake! He got on his bicycle and rode swiftly away, the other six following.

They all stopped outside the tea-shop.

'Whew!' said Peter, wiping his forehead. 'I DID feel awful when I found out he was a friend of my father's! Dad is always talking about a man called Harry, but I didn't know his surname before.'

'We thought we were so clever, but we weren't this time,' said Colin. 'Blow! The spectacle case was nothing to do with those two men in the car, but perhaps the button is?'

'Perhaps,' said Peter. 'But I'm not tackling anyone wearing macs with buttons that match the one we found, unless I'm jolly certain he's one of those men! I feel hot all over when I think of Mr Briggs. Suppose he goes and tells my father all about this?'

'Never mind,' said Jack, grinning. 'It was great fun watching you. Let's have tea. Look, they've got macaroons today.'

In they went and had a wonderful tea. And now, what next? Think hard, Secret Seven, and make some exciting plans!

Eleven

Jobs for every member

THE next day another Secret Seven meeting was held, but this time it was at Colin's, in his little summer-house. It wasn't such a good place as Peter's shed, because it had an open doorway with no door, and they were not allowed to have an oil-stove in it.

However, Colin's mother had asked all the Secret Seven to tea, so it was clear they would have to have their next meeting at his house, and the little summer-house was the only place where they could talk in secret.

'We'll bring all our fireworks and look through them,' said Peter. 'We haven't so much as *glanced* at them the last two meetings, and it's Bonfire Night in a few days. We simply MUST see what we've got and what we haven't got.'

So all the Secret Seven went laden with fireworks to Colin's house. They had a fine tea, the kind they all enjoyed most.

'Sardine sandwiches, honey sandwiches, a smashing cherry cake with cherries inside *and* on top, and an iced sponge cake. I say, Colin, your mother's a jolly good sort,' said Peter, approvingly. 'Isn't she going to have it with us? I'd like to thank her.'

'No, she's had to go out to a committee meeting or

something,' said Colin. 'All she said was that we've to behave ourselves, and if we go down to the summer-house this cold dark evening, we've GOT to put on our coats.'

'Right,' said Peter. 'Coats it will be. Mothers are always very keen on coats, aren't they? Personally, I think it's quite hot today.'

They finished up absolutely everything on the tea-table. There wasn't even a piece of the big cherry cake left! Scamper, who had also been asked to tea, had his own dish of dog-biscuits with shrimp paste on each. He was simply delighted, and crunched them up non-stop.

'Now we'll go to the summer-house. We'd better take a candle it's so dark already,' said Colin. 'And don't forget your coats, everyone!'

'And the fireworks,' said Peter.

So down they all went to the little wooden summer-house, carrying their fireworks. The house had a wooden bench running all round it, and smelt a bit damp. Nobody minded that. It was such a nice secret place to talk in, down at the bottom of the dark garden.

The candle was stuck in a bottle and lighted. There was no shelf to put it on, so Colin stood it in the middle of the floor.

'Have to be careful of Scamper knocking it over!' said Peter. 'Where is he?'

'He's gone into the kitchen to see our cook,' said Colin. 'She's cooking a stew or something, and Scamper smelt it. He'll be along soon. Now, stack the fireworks under the wooden bench for the time being. That's right. We'll go through them when we've had the meeting.'

'We'll begin it now,' said Peter. 'Owing to our silly mistake about the spectacle case, were not as far on with this adventure as we ought to be. We must do a little more work on it. First, has anyone any idea where "Sid's place" is?'

There was a silence.

'Never heard of it,' said Jack.

'Well, it must be some place that is used by men like those two in my father's car,' said Peter.

'Perhaps Larry at the garage would know?' said Colin, who had great faith in Larry. 'He knows a lot of lorry-drivers, and they're the kind who might go to some place called "Sid's" or "Jim's" or "Nick's".'

'Yes. That's a good idea,' said Peter. 'Colin, you and George go and find out from Larry tomorrow. Now, what else can we do? What about the number that one of the men had to get in touch with – what was it now?'

'Q8061,' said Pam, promptly. 'I think of it as the *letter* Q, but it might be spelt K-E-W, you know.'

'Yes, you're right. It might,' said Peter. 'That's really quite an idea, Pam. It might be a telephone number at Kew telephone exchange, Kew 8061. You and Barbara can make it your job to find out.'

'How do we set about it?' said Barbara.

'I really can't explain such easy things to you,' said

Peter, impatiently. 'You and Pam can quite well work out what to do yourselves. Now is there anything else we can work on?'

'Only the button we found in the car,' said Jack.

'I told you, it's sure to belong to my father's mac,' said Peter. 'It's just like the buttons on it.'

'But we ought to make *sure*,' argued Jack. 'You know you always say we never ought to leave anything to chance, Peter. There are hundreds of different coat buttons.'

'Well perhaps you're right,' said Peter. 'Yes, I think you are. Janet, will you see to that point, please, and look at Dad's mac. I know he's got a button missing, so I expect it belongs to his mac, but we *will* make sure.'

'You haven't given *me* anything to do,' said Jack.

'Well, if the button doesn't match the ones on Dad's mac, you can take charge of *that* point,' said Peter, with a sudden giggle, 'and you can march about looking for people wearing a mac with a missing button.'

'Don't be an ass,' said Jack. 'Still, if it *isn't* your father's button, it *will* be one dropped by one of those men, and one of us ought to take charge of it. So I will, if it's necessary.'

'Right,' said Peter. 'Well, that's the end of the meeting. Now we'll get out the fireworks!'

Twelve

Oh, what a pity!

COLIN and Jack took the bundles of fireworks out from under the wooden bench of the summer-house. The Seven then knelt down on the floor to undo the parcels and the boxes. What a lovely job!

'I wish we had a better light than just this flickering candle on the floor,' said Pam. 'It's difficult to read the names of the fireworks!'

As they all bent over the fireworks by the light of the candle, they heard the sound of a bark, and then scampering feet. Scamper had been let out of the kitchen door and was coming to find his friends. Where were they? Wuff! Wuff!

'Scamper!' called Janet from the summer-house. 'We're here!'

Scamper tore down the garden path, barking madly. Anyone would think he had been away from the seven children for a whole month, not just half an hour!

He rushed straight into the little summer-house and over went the bottle with the lighted candle in its neck! Crash!

'You idiot, Scamper,' said Peter and reached to set the bottle upright again. The candle was still alight.

155

But before he could take hold of it, the flame of the candle had licked against a bundle of fireworks. They were alight! And not only were they alight, but they were fizzing and spluttering!

'They're going off!' yelled Peter. 'Look out, Pam, look out, Barbara!'

Fizzzzzz! Pop-pop-pop! BANG!

Half a dozen fireworks went off together, and the seven children and Scamper tumbled hurried out of the little summer-house, trying to get out of the way.

The loose paper on the floor had now been set alight too, and in its turn it set fire to a pile of small fireworks, rather like squibs.

Bang-popbang-popbang-bang! They all went off too. The children clutched one another in dismay. Scamper, really terrified, had completely disappeared.

BANG! BANG! WHOOOOOOSH!

A rocket flew out of the summer-house, and Colin only just got back out of its way in time. Peter dragged everyone back, and Colin fell into a holly bush and yelled so loud that everyone thought the rocket must have hit him.

'Can't we save the rest of the fireworks?' cred Jack, dismayed at seeing all their precious bundles going up in smoke and flame and bangs.

'No. Not unless you want to be smothered in Rockets, and Squibs, and Blue-Flashes, and Whirligigs – and, oh my goodness, what was that?' yelled Peter.

'My Humdinger! My Humdinger!' wailed poor Jack, as something with a long fiery tail flew out of the summer-house with a loud roar. 'It cost me thirty pence!'

'I say, we'd better get some water,' said Colin, suddenly. 'The summer-house might get on fire. Look at that paper blazing up.'

They left the firework show and ran to get buckets. There was a little pond nearby, and they filled the buckets from it. Splash! Splash! Splash! The water was thrown all over the blazing fireworks, and there was a tremendous sizzling noise. Black smoke poured out of the little house and almost choked the Seven.

'Pooh!' said Jack, and coughed. 'What a horrible smell!'

'It's a good thing your mother's out,' panted Peter to Colin, coming up with another pail of water. 'She would be in a frightful way about this. There, I think we've about got the fire down now. Poooooh! That smoke!'

It was a very, very sad ending to the tea and meeting at Colin's. Barbara was in tears. She had saved up for weeks to buy fireworks, and now there was nothing left of them but smoke and smell and a nasty-looking black mess.

'It's bad luck,' said Peter, feeling as if he wouldn't mind howling himself. 'Blow Scamper! It's all his fault. Where is he?'

'Gone home at sixty miles an hour, I should think,' said Janet. 'It's a pity he hasn't got a post-office savings book like we have. I'd make him take a whole lot of money out and buy more fireworks for us. It's too bad. We shan't have any now!'

'Well we certainly shan't be able to buy enough to make a display,' said Jack, gloomily. 'Come on, let's go. Sorry, Colin, about making your summer-house in a mess. I'll come along tomorrow, when it's dried up a bit, and help you to clear it up.'

They were just about to go off to the front gate when Janet stopped them. 'We meant to choose a new password today,' she said. 'You know that Susie knows our last one, "Guy Fawkes", and we really *must* have a secret one. Susie has told everyone in our class.'

'Yes. I forgot about that,' said Peter. 'Well, I vote we have "Fireworks". It really does seem a very good password for tonight!'

'All right – Fireworks,' said Colin. 'I'm sorry its been such a disappointing evening. This is definitely *not* the kind of adventure I like! Goodbye, all of you. See you tomorrow!'

It was a gloomy company of children that made their way home. Blow Scamper, *why* did he have to do a silly thing like that?

Thirteen

Sid's Place

ALL the Secret Seven felt exceedingly gloomy next day, which was Sunday. They met at Sunday School, but none of them had much to say. They were all very subdued. It really was a dreadful thing to have seen weeks and weeks of savings going up in smoke in just a few minutes!

'Scamper *did* race home last night,' said Janet to the girls. 'He was behind the couch, trembling from head to foot. He is awfully frightened of fireworks, you know.'

'All dogs are,' said Pam. 'We always lock ours up indoors on Bonfire Night. Poor Scamper! Did you forgive him?'

'We simply had to,' said Janet. 'Anyway, he didn't mean to upset the candle, poor Scamper. We stroked him and patted him and loved him, and when he saw we weren't going to scold him, he crept out and sat as close to our legs as he could, and put his head on my knee.'

'He's a dear,' said Barbara. 'But all the same it's *dreadful* to have lost all our fireworks at one go.'

'It's quite put our adventure out of my mind,' said Pam. 'But I suppose we'd better think about it again tomorrow, Barbara. We've got to find out about that telephone number, Kew 8061. Though how we shall do it, I don't know.'

'Leave it till tomorrow,' said Barbara. 'I can't think of anything but our poor fireworks today.'

The next day was Monday, and the Seven were back at school. George and Colin went to call at the garage after morning school, to try and find out something about 'Sid's Place' from Larry. He was sitting in a corner with a newspaper, munching his lunch.

'Hallo, Larry,' said Colin. 'I wonder if you can help us. Do you know anywhere called "Sid's Place"?'

'No, I don't,' said Larry. 'Sounds like an eating-house or something. There's a lorry-driver coming in soon. If you like to wait, I'll ask him.'

The lorry drove in after three or four minutes, and the man got down, a big heavy fellow who called out cheerfully to Larry. 'Just off to get a bite of dinner. Be back in half an hour for my lorry.'

'Hey, Charlie, do you eat at "Sid's Place"?' called Larry. 'Do you know it?'

' "Sid's Place"? No, I eat at my sisters when I come through here,' said Charlie. 'Wait a minute now. "Sid's" you said. Yes I remember seeing a little café called "Sid's Café". Would that be the place you're meaning?'

'Could be,' said Larry, looking questioningly at Colin.

Colin nodded. 'Probably the one,' he said, feeling suddenly excited. 'Where is it?'

'You know Old Street? Well, it's at the corner of

Old Street and James Street, not a first-class place, and not the sort you boys want to go to. So long, Larry. See you in half an hour!'

'Thanks, Larry,' said Colin. 'Come on, George, let's go and have a look at this place. We've just about got time.'

They went to Old Street and walked down to James Street at the end. On the corner, sharing a bit of each street, was a rather dirty-looking eating-house. 'Sid's Café' was painted over the top of the very messy window.

The boys looked inside. Men were sitting at a long counter, eating sandwiches and drinking coffee or tea. There were one or two tables in the shop, too, at which slightly better-dressed men were having a hot meal served to them by a fat and cheerful girl.

'Oh so that's "Sid's Place",' said Colin, staring in. 'I wonder which is Sid?'

'Perhaps Sid is somewhere in the back quarters,' said George. 'There are only girls serving here. Well we know that one of those men comes here every day about five o'clock. One of us must watch, and we'll be bound to see the man.'

'It'll have to be Peter,' said Colin. 'We wouldn't know the fellow. He would probably recognize him at once.'

'Yes. It's going to be jolly difficult for him to hang about here, watching everyone,' said George. 'People will wonder what he's up to. Two of us would seem even *more* suspicious.'

'Well that's up to Peter!' said Colin. 'We've done *our* job and found Sid's place. Come on, we'll be awfully late for lunch.'

Peter was very pleased with Colin and George when he heard their news. 'Good work!' he said. 'I'll get along there at five o'clock this afternoon. How have Pam and Barbara got on?'

Janet told him while they had a quick tea together after afternoon school. 'They simply couldn't think *how* to do anything about KEW 8061,' said Janet. 'They simply couldn't.'

'Couple of idiots!' said Peter, munching a bun quickly. 'Buck up, I must go.'

'Well, Pam asked her mother how to find out if there *was* such a number, because she and Barbara really didn't feel they could wade all through the telephone directories,' said Janet. 'And her mother said, "Well, just ring up and see if there's an answer!" '

'Easy,' said Peter. 'Simple!'

'Yes – well, they rang up the number, feeling frightfully excited, because they thought they could ask whoever answered what his name and address were, but there was no reply,' said Janet. 'And the operator said it was because there was no telephone with that number at present! So Q8061 is *not* a telephone number, Peter. It must be something else.'

'Blow!' said Peter, getting up. 'It would have been marvellous if KEW 8061 *had* answered. We'd have been able to get the name and address and everything. That clue isn't much good, I'm afraid. I must be off, Janet. Wouldn't it be wonderful if I spotted one of the men going into Sid's place?'

'It *would*,' said Janet. 'Oh, I DO hope you do, Peter!'

Fourteen

A wonderful idea

PETER went as quickly as he could to the corner of
Old Street and James Street. Yes – there was 'Sid's
Cafè', just as Colin had said. What was the time?

He glanced at his watch – six minutes to five. Well,
if the man came at five o'clock, he ought just to catch
him. Of course, he might come any time after that.
That would be a nuisance, because then Peter would
have to wait about a long time.

Peter lolled against the corner, watching everyone
who came by, especially, of course, the men who went
in and out of 'Sid's Cafè'. They were mostly men with
barrows of fruit that they left outside, or drivers of
vans, or shifty-looking men, unshaved and dirty.

He got a shock when someone came out of the café
and spoke roughly to him.

'Now then, what are you doing here, lolling about?
Don't you dare take fruit off my barrow! I've caught
you boys doing it before, and I'll call the police if you
do. Clear off!'

'I wouldn't *dream* of taking your fruit!' said Peter,
indignantly, looking at the pile of cheap fruit on the
nearby barrow.

'Ho, you wouldn't, would you? Well, then, what
are you standing here for, looking about? Boys don't

stand at corners for nothing! We've been watching
you from inside the shop, me and my mates, and we
know you're after something!'

Peter was shocked. How dare this man say things
like that to him! Still, perhaps boys in this district did
steal from barrows or from fruit-stalls outside
shops.

'Go on, you tell me what you're standing about here for,' said the man again, putting his face close to Peter's.

As the boy couldn't tell him the reason why he was standing at that corner, he said nothing, but turned and went off, his face burning red. Horrible man! he thought. And I haven't seen anyone yet in the least like that fellow who went off in our car. Of course, all I've got to go on really is his hat and long hair, and possibly maimed finger on his right hand.

He ran back home, thinking hard. After all, that fellow might go to Sid's place each night and I'd *never* know him if he had a cap instead of a hat, and had cut his hair shorter. And most of these fellows slouch along with their hands in their pockets, so I wouldn't see his hand either. It's hopeless.

Peter went round to see Colin about it. Jack and George were there, doing their homework together.

'Hallo!' they said, in surprise. 'Aren't you watching at Sid's place?'

Peter told them what had happened. 'I don't see how I can go and watch there any more,' he said, rather gloomily. 'That fellow who spoke to me was really nasty. And how can I watch without being seen?'

'Can't be done,' said Colin. 'Give it up! This is something we just can't do. Come on out to the summer-house and see what I've made! We cleared away the firework mess, and I've got something else there now!'

They all went out to the summer-house, with their torches. Colin shone his on to something there, and Peter jumped in astonishment, not at first realizing what it was.

'Gosh! It's a guy!' he said, in admiration. 'What a beauty!'

The guy certainly was very fine. He was stuffed with straw, and wore one of Colin's very old suits. He had a mask, of course, and grinned happily at the three boys. He had a wig made of black strands of wool and an old hat on top. Colin had sat him in a garden barrow, and he really looked marvellous.

'I thought that as we shan't have many fireworks, worse luck, we would have a guy and burn him on a bonfire,' said Colin. 'I'm making the bonfire heap tomorrow. You can come and help if you like.'

The guy seemed to watch them as they talked, grinning away merrily.

'It's a pity *he* can't watch outside Sid's place!' said Jack. 'Nobody would suspect him or bother about *him*. He could watch for that fellow all evening!'

They all laughed. Then Peter stopped suddenly and gazed hard at the guy. An idea had come to him, a really WONDERFUL idea!

'I say! I SAY!' he said, clutching at Colin and making him jump. 'You've given me an idea! What about ME dressing up as a guy, and wearing a mask with eye-holes – and one of you taking me somewhere near Sid's Café? There are heaps of these guys about now, and nobody would think our guy was *real.*

I could watch for ages and nobody would guess.'

'Whew!' said the other three together, and stared at Peter in admiration.

Colin thumped him on the back. 'That's a wizard idea!' he said. 'Super! Smashing! When shall we do it?'

'Tomorrow,' said Peter. 'I can rush here and dress up easily enough, and one of you can wheel me off in the barrow – all of you, if you like! What a game!'

'But my mother doesn't like the idea of children taking guys and begging for money,' said Colin, remembering. 'She says that begging is wrong.'

'So it is,' said Peter. 'My mother says that too, but if we *did* get any money we could give it to a charity. We won't use it to buy fireworks for ourselves.'

'Oh well, that's all right, then!' said Colin. 'My word, this is grand! Mind you don't leap up out of the barrow if you see that fellow going into Sid's place, Peter!'

'I'll keep as still as a real guy!' said Peter, grinning. 'Well, so long. See you at school tomorrow.'

Fifteen

The peculiar guy

PETER raced home to tell Janet of the new idea. She was so thrilled that she couldn't say a word. What an idea! How super! She stared in admiration at her brother. He was truly a fine leader for the Secret Seven!

Scamper wuffed loudly, exactly as if he were saying, 'Grand, Peter, splendid idea!'

'*I've* got something to tell you, too,' said Janet, suddenly remembering. 'I looked on Daddy's macintosh and he *has* got a button missing; but it's a small one on his sleeve, not a large one like we found. And also it's not quite the same colour, Peter.'

'Ah, good! That means it probably *was* a button that dropped from that fellow's mac!' said Peter, pleased. 'Jack will have to take the button, Janet, and work on that clue, if he can! So give it to me, and I'll hand it to him tomorrow.'

'I wish we could find out about Q8061,' said Janet. 'I'm pretty sure it must be someone's telephone number, but it's very difficult to find out.'

'There's Mother calling,' said Peter. 'I bet it's to tell me to do my homework!'

It was of course, and poor Peter found it very difficult indeed to work out arithmetic problems when his head was full of dressing up as a guy!

All the Secret Seven were thrilled to hear of Peter's new plan, and next evening they were round at Colin's to see him dress up. He really did look remarkably good!

He wore an old pair of patched trousers, and a ragged jacket. He wore a pair of great big boots thrown out by Colin's father. He had a scarf round his neck, and a big old hat over a wig made of black wool.

'You look simply *frightful!*' said Janet, with a giggle. 'Put the mask on now.'

Peter put it on, and immediately became a grinning guy, like all the other guys that were appearing here and there in the streets of the town. Scamper took one look at Peter's suddenly changed face, and backed away, growling.

'It's all right, Scamper,' said Peter, laughing. 'It's me! Don't be afraid.'

'You look horrible,' said Pam. 'I really feel scared when I look at you, though I know you're really Peter. Nobody, *nobody* could possibly guess you were alive!'

Peter got into the barrow. 'Gosh, it's very hard and uncomfortable,' he said. 'Got any old cushions, Colin?'

Colin produced an old rug and three rather dirty garden cushions. These made the barrow much more comfortable. Peter got in and lolled on the cushions in the limp, floppy way of all guys. He really looked extremely guy-like!

The others shrieked with laughter to see him.

'Come on,' said Colin at last. 'We really must go, or we shan't be there till long past five. Not you girls. It's not a place for you, outside Sid's Café.'

The three boys set off, taking turns at wheeling Peter in the barrow. He kept making horrible groans and moans, and Jack laughed so much that he had to sit down on a bus-stop seat and hold his aching sides.

An old lady there peered at the guy. 'What a good one!' she said, and fumbled in her purse. I'll give you some money to buy fireworks.'

'Oh, any money we get is going to charity,' explained George quickly.

She gave him ten pence, and then, as the bus came up, waved to them and got on.

'How nice of her!' said George. 'Ten whole pence.'

They went on down the street, with Peter thoroughly enjoying himself! He lolled about, watching everything through the eye-slits of his mask, and made silly remarks in a hollow, guy-like voice that made the others laugh helplessly.

At last they came to Sid's Café. The barrow was neatly wedged into a little alcove near the door, from which Peter could see everyone who went in or out.

The boys stood nearby, waiting to see if Peter recognized anyone. If he did, he was to give a sign, and two of the Seven would shadow the man to see where he went, if he happened to come *out* of the café. If he went inside it they were to wait till he came out.

The men going in and out of the eating-house were
amused with the guy. One prodded him hard with his
stick, and gave Peter a terrible shock. 'Good guy
you've got there!' said the man and threw five pence
on to Peter's tummy.

'Colin! Jack! You're NOT to let people prod me like
that,' said Peter, in a fierce whisper. 'It jolly well
hurt.'

'Well, how are we to stop them?' said Colin, also in
a whisper.

All went well till two young fellows came by and saw the guy sitting there. 'Hallo! He's a good guy!' said one. 'Nice pair of boots he's got. I've a good mind to take them off him!'

And to Peter's horror, he felt the boots on his feet being tugged hard. He gave a yell, and the young fellows looked extremely startled. They disappeared quickly.

'CAN'T you look after me better?' said Peter to the others. 'Heave me up a bit on the cushions. Those fellows pulled me off.'

Colin and George heaved him into a more comfortable position.

'Anyway, you've made quite a bit of money,' said George, in Peter's ear. 'People think you're jolly good, we've got quite a few pence, and some silver.'

Peter grunted. He was cross with the others. Why didn't they guard him from pokes and prods and pullings? Then, quite suddenly, he caught sight of somebody, and stiffened all over.

'Surely, SURELY, that was one of the men who had taken his father's car? Peter stared and stared. Was it? Oh, why didn't he stand a bit nearer so that he could see?

Sixteen

The two men

THE man was standing by the window of the café, as if he were waiting for someone. He had on a hat and his hair was rather long. Peter looked as closely at him as he could.

The fellow who drove the car had a low-brimmed hat, he thought and long hair. This man somehow *looks* like that man we saw in the car.

The man moved a little nearer, and coughed impatiently. He took a cigarette packet from his pocket and pulled out a cigarette. He turned away from the wind and towards Peter in order to light it, and then Peter knew for *certain* that it was the man he was looking for!

The top of his middle finger is missing! he thought. I saw it clearly in the flame of the match as he lighted his cigarette. It *must* be the fellow! Perhaps he's waiting for the other man.

Almost before he had finished thinking this, the second man came up! There was no mistaking that cap and the short, cropped hair, grown a little longer now. The cap was pulled down over his face exactly as it had been when he was in the car. He wore an old macintosh, and Peter tried to see if it had a button missing.

The two men said a word of greeting and then went into the café. They went right through the room to a door at the back, opened it, and disappeared.

'Colin! George! Jack! Those were the two men,' called Peter in a low voice full of excitement. 'One of them had half a finger missing. I saw it.'

'And the other had a button off his mac!' said Jack. 'I noticed that, though I didn't know he was one of the men we're after! But seeing that I'm in charge of the button now, I'm making a point of looking carefully at every macintosh I see! I believe our button matches his exactly.'

'Good work!' said Peter. 'Now listen. The next move is very, very important. Two of you must shadow these men. If they separate, you must separate too, and each go after one of them. Colin, you must wheel me home.'

'Right,' said the three, always willing to obey Peter's leadership. He really was very good at this kind of thing.

'Get as close to those men as you can and see if you can hear anything useful,' said Peter. 'And track them right to their homes if you can. Report to me at the Secret Seven shed as soon as you can.'

'Right,' said George and Jack, feeling as if they were first-class plain-clothes policemen!

The two men were not long in Sid's. They came out after about ten minutes, looking angry. They stood in the doorway, taking no notice of the guy and the boys.

'Sid's let us down,' said the man with the missing finger. 'He said he'd give us two hundred and now he's knocked it down to fifty. Better go back to Q's and tell him. He'll be wild.'

The boys listened intently, pretending to fiddle about with the guy.

'I'm not arguing with Sid again,' said the other man. 'I reckon I'm an idiot to come out of hiding, yet, till my hair's grown. Come on, let's go.'

They went off down the street, and George and Jack immediately set off behind them, leaving Colin with Peter.

'Did you hear that?' said Peter, in great excitement, forgetting he was a guy. 'They've stolen something and want to sell it to Sid, and he won't give them what he promised. So they're going back to Q, whoever he is, probably the chief, to report it. Well we know that Q is a man, now!'

'And did you hear what the other fellow said about his hair growing?' said Colin, bending over Peter. 'I bet he's just come out of prison, it's so short. They always shave it there, don't they? Or perhaps he's an *escaped* prisoner, in hiding. Gosh, Peter, this is super!'

'Wheel me to our shed,' commanded Peter, wishing he could get out and walk. 'Buck up. The girls will be there already, and George and Jack will join us as soon as they can. Do buck up! .... I'm going to get out and walk,' announced Peter. 'It's a nice dark road we're in. Stop a minute, Colin, and I'll get out.'

Colin stopped, and Peter climbed out of the
barrow. Colin shone his torch to help him, and an old
man with a dog saw the guy stepping out of the
barrow. He stared as if he couldn't believe his eyes,
and then hurried off at top speed. Good gracious! A
guy coming alive. No, surely his eyes must have de-
ceived him!

It wasn't long before Colin and Peter were whispering the password outside the shed at the bottom of

Peter's garden. The barrow was shoved into some bushes, and Peter had taken off his mask.

'Fireworks!' said the boys, and the door opened at once. Pam gave a little scream as Peter came in, still looking very peculiar with a black wool wig, an old hat, and very ragged clothes.

'We've got news!' said Peter. 'Grand news. Just listen, all of you!'

Seventeen

Good work!

PETER quickly told the girls all that had happened, and they listened in silence, feeling very thrilled. Now they were really finding out something, and even that button had helped!

'I think the short-haired man has either just come out of prison or escaped from it,' said Peter. 'He may have committed a robbery before he went in, and have hidden what he stole, and it's these goods he and the other fellow are trying to sell to Sid.'

'Well, who's Q, then?' asked Janet. 'Where does *he* come in?'

'He's probably holding the stolen goods,' said Peter, working everything out in his mind. 'And I expect he's sheltering the thief, too. If only we could find out who Q is and where he lives. He's the missing link.'

The five of them talked and talked, and Scamper listened and joined in with a few wuffs now and again, thumping his tail on the ground when the chatter got very loud.

'When will George and Jack be back?' asked Pam. 'I ought not to be too late home, and it's a quarter past six now!'

'Here they are!' said Colin, hearing voices outside. A knock came at the door.

'Password!' shouted everyone.

'Fireworks!' said two voices, and in went George and Jack, beaming all over their faces, glad to be out of the cold, dark November night.

'What happened? Did you shadow them?' demanded Peter, as they sat down on boxes.

'Yes,' said George. 'We followed them all the way down the street, and away by the canal and up by Cole Square. We only once got near enough to hear them say anything.'

'What was that?' asked Peter.

'One of them said "Is that a policeman lying in wait for us over there? Come on, run for it!"' said George. 'And just as a bobby came out of the shadows they ran round the corner, and the policeman never even noticed them! We shot after them, just in time to see them trying the handles of some cars parked there.'

'Then they slid quickly into one and drove off,' finished Jack. 'That was the end of our shadowing.'

'So they stole *another* car!' said Colin.

'You didn't take the number by any chance, did you?' asked Peter.

'Rather!' said Jack, and took out his notebook. 'Here it is, PLK 100. We didn't go back and tell the policeman. We thought we'd race back here and let you decide what we ought to do next.'

'Good work,' said Peter, pleased. 'If only we knew where Q lived, we'd know where the men were, and could tell the police to go and grab them there.

They'd get the stolen goods too. I bet they're being held by our mysterious Q!'

'I know! I know!' suddenly yelled Pam, making everyone jump. 'Why can't we look up all the names beginning with Q in our local telephone directory? If Q lives somewhere here, his name would be there, and his number.'

'Yes but there might be a lot of Q's, and we wouldn't know which was the right one,' objected Janet. 'Why, we ourselves know a Mrs Queen, a Mr Quigley and a Miss Quorn.'

'But don't you see what I *mean*!' said Pam, impatiently. 'We'll go down all the list of Q's, and the one with the telephone number of 8061 will be *our* Q! Don't you *see*?'

Everyone saw what she meant at once.

Peter looked at Pam admiringly. 'That's a very good idea, Pam,' he said. 'I've sometimes thought that you're not as good a Secret Seven member as the others are, but now I know you are. That's a Very Good Idea. Why didn't we think of it before instead of messing about with K.E.W.?'

'I'll get our telephone directory with all the numbers in,' said Janet and raced off.

She soon came back, gave the password and joined the others. She opened the book at the Q's, and everyone craned to look at them.

There were not very many. 'Quant,' read Pam, 'telephone number 6015. Queen, 6453, Quelling, 4322, Quentin, 8061. . . . ! That's it. Look, here it is,

Quentin, 8061, Barr's Warehouse East End. Why, that's only about two miles away, right at the other end of the town!'

'My WORD!' said Peter, delighted. 'That's given us JUST the information we wanted. A warehouse, too. A fine place for hiding stolen goods! My goodness, we've done some jolly good work. Pam, you deserve a pat on the back!'

She got plenty of pats, and sat back, beaming. 'What do we do now?' she said.

Before anyone could answer, there came the sound of footsteps down the path, and Peter's mother's voice called loudly: 'Peter! Janet! Are Colin and George there, and Pam? Their mothers have just telephoned to say they really must come home at once, it's getting late!'

'Right, Mummy!' called Peter. 'Wait for us. We've got a wonderful tale to tell you! Do wait!'

But his mother had gone scurrying back to the house, not liking the cold, damp evening. The seven children tore after her, with Scamper barking his head off.

Just as they went in at the back of the house, there came a knock at the front door.

'See who that is, Peter!' called his mother. 'I've got a cake in the oven I must look at.'

Peter went to the door, with the others close behind him. A big policeman stood there. He smiled at the surprised children.

'I've just been to Master Jack's house,' he said, 'and Miss Susie told me he might be here. I saw you tonight in Cole Square – you and this other boy here. Well, not long after that somebody reported to me that their car had been stolen near where you were, and I wondered if either of you had noticed anything suspicious going on.'

'Oh, come in, come in!' cried Peter, joyfully. 'We can tell you a whole lot about the thieves, and we can even tell you where you'll probably find the car. Come in, do!'

Eighteen

Don't worry, Secret Seven!

THE policeman went into the hall, looking extremely surprised. Peter's mother came from the kitchen and Peter's father looked out of his study.

'What's all this?' he said. 'Nobody has got into trouble, surely?'

'No,' said Peter. 'Oh, Daddy, you must just listen to our tale. It's really super!'

They all went into the study, the policeman looking more and more puzzled.

'I *think* you'll find that stolen car outside Barr's Warehouse, at the East End of the town,' said Peter. 'And in the warehouse you'll probably find a Mr Quentin, and quite a lot of stolen goods on the premises.'

'And you'll find a man with half a finger missing, and another whose hair is so short that he looks like an escaped prisoner,' put in Colin.

'Wait! Wait a minute! What's this about a man with a missing half-finger?' said the policeman, urgently. 'We're looking for him – Fingers, he's called, and he's a friend of a thief who's just been in prison. He escaped last week, and we thought he might go to Fingers for help, so we've been keeping an eye open for him too.'

'They met at Sid's Café,' said Peter, enjoying everyone's astonishment.

'WHAT?' said his father. 'Sid's Café? That horrible place! Don't dare to tell me you boys have been in there.'

'Not inside, only outside,' said Peter. 'It's all right, Daddy. We *really* haven't done anything wrong. It all began with that night when you left Janet and me in your car in the station yard, and two men got in and drove it away.'

'And we wanted you to go to the police, but you didn't think you'd bother,' said Janet. 'So we've been trying to trace the two men ourselves, and we have!'

Then the whole of the story came out how they found Sid's Café, how Peter dressed up as a guy to watch for the men, how they saw Fingers with his missing half-finger, and how George and Jack followed them and saw them steal the car near Cole Square.

'And we know where they've gone, because they have a friend called Q, a Mr Quentin,' said Peter. 'They mentioned his telephone number, it was 8061, and we looked up the number and found the address. We only did that a little while ago, actually. The address is Barr's Warehouse, as we said.'

'Amazing!' said the policeman, scribbling fast in his note-book. 'Incredible! Do these kids do this kind of thing often, sir?'

'Well, you're a fairly new man here,' said Peter's father, 'or you'd know how they keep poking their

noses into all sorts of things. I don't know that I really approve of it, but they certainly have done some good work.'

'We're the Secret Seven Society, you see,' explained Janet. 'And we really do like some kind of adventurous job to do.'

'Well, thanks very much,' said the policeman, getting up. 'I'll get a few men and ask the Sergeant to come along with us and see what we can find in Barr's Warehouse. You'll deserve a jolly good Bonfire Night tomorrow! I hope you've got a wonderful collection of fireworks, you deserve the best!'

'Well, actually we've hardly any,' said Peter. 'We collected masses, but they all went up in a fire last Saturday, quite by accident. It was dreadful.'

'That was very bad luck,' said the policeman, going to the door. 'I'm much obliged to you all. Good night, madam; good night, sir!'

'What a tale!' said Peter's mother. 'I never heard of such goings-on! Whatever will you Seven do next? To think of you dressing up as a guy, Peter, and watching outside Sid's Café! No wonder you look so DREADFUL! Take that black wig off, do!

'Mummy, *can't* the others stay and have a bit of supper?' begged Peter. 'We've got such a lot to talk about. Do let them. Sandwiches will do. We'll all help to make them.'

'Very well,' said his mother, laughing at all the excited faces. 'Janet, go and telephone everybody's mothers and tell them where they are!'

The Seven were very pleased. In fifteen minutes' time they were all sitting down to potted meat sandwiches, oatmeal biscuits, apples and hot cocoa, talking nineteen to the dozen, with a very excited Scamper tearing round their legs under the table. What an unexpected party! thought Scamper, delighted, and what a wonderful selection of titbits!

The telephone suddenly rang, and Peter went to answer it. It proved to be a very exciting call indeed! He came racing back to the others.

'That was that policeman! He thought we'd like to know what happened.'

'What? Tell us!' cried everyone.

'Well, the police went to Barr's Warehouse and the first thing they saw in the yard was the stolen car!' said Peter. 'Then they forced their way in at a back door, and found Mr Quentin, scared stiff, in his office. When they told him they knew that Fingers and the escaped prisoner were somewhere in the warehouse, he just crumpled up!'

'Have they got the others?' asked Colin.

'Oh yes. Quentin showed the police where they were hiding,' said Peter. 'Down in a cellar, and the stolen goods were there too. It was a wonderful raid! By the way, the police want to know if we can identify the second man, the close-cropped man, and I said yes, if he was wearing a mac with a missing button, because we've got the button!'

Goody, goody!' said Barbara. 'So we have. We

forgot to tell the policeman about that! Where *is* the button?'

'Here,' said Jack, and spun it on the table. 'Good old button, you did your bit too! My word, this is one of the most exciting jobs the Secret Seven have ever done. I'm jolly sorry it's ended.'

So was everyone. They didn't want that exciting evening to come to a finish, but they had to say good-bye at last.

'There's only one thing that's spoilt this adventure,' said Peter to Janet, as they shut the front door on the others. 'That's the burning-up of our fireworks, and tomorrow is Bonfire Night. What a shame!'

But don't worry, Secret Seven, there's a parcel on the way to you, being brought by your friend the policeman. What's inside? Ah, you'll never guess!

It's a reward from the police for all your good work – two hundred wonderful fireworks of all kinds. Just wait till you see them, you'll hardly believe your eyes.

BANG! WHOOSH! BANG-BANG-BANG! What a lovely end to a most exciting story!